THE BIG BOOK OF ANIMAL STORIES

Ruskin Bond has been writing for over sixty years, and has now over 120 titles in print—novels, collections of stories, poetry, essays, anthologies and books for children. His first novel, *The Room on the Roof*, received the prestigious John Llewellyn Rhys Award in 1957. He has also received the Padma Shri (1999), the Padma Bhushan (2014) and two awards from the Sahitya Akademi—one for his short stories and another for his writings for children. In 2012, the Delhi government gave him its Lifetime Achievement Award.

Born in 1934, Ruskin Bond grew up in Jamnagar, Shimla, New Delhi and Dehradun. Apart from three years in the UK, he has spent all his life in India, and now lives in Mussoorie with his adopted family.

A shy person, Ruskin says he likes being a writer because 'When I'm writing there's nobody watching me. Today, it's hard to find a profession where you're not being watched!'

D1603798

THE BIG BOOK OF ANIMAL STORIES

RUSKIN BOND

RUPA

Published by
Rupa Publications India Pvt. Ltd 2015
7/16, Ansari Road, Daryaganj
New Delhi 110002

Sales Centres:

Allahabad Bengaluru Chennai
Hyderabad Jaipur Kathmandu
Kolkata Mumbai

ISBN: 978-81-291-3714-2

First impression 2015

10 9 8 7 6 5 4 3 2 1

The moral right of the author has been asserted.

Printed by Thomson Press India Ltd., Faridabad

Contents

Introduction

I like animals and get on well with most of them (barring crocodiles and big cats), but I would be dishonest if I called myself a great animal lover. I do not enjoy being licked by dogs, scratched by kittens or having my nose tweaked by a parrot. House pets are not my cup of tea. Let birds and animals roam the wilds, and I will help to protect the wilds for them.

Why, then, have I written so many animals stories?

Well, I'll tell you a professional secret.

In the good old, bad old days, when I was in my twenties and thirties, I wasn't making much money from my writing. And I felt I had to do something different, even if only for a certain period of time. So I looked at all the magazines and Sunday papers and popular books, and discovered that many of them carried animal stories, either of cute, cuddly animals or of wild creatures, ready to tear you to pieces. So, I thought, why not write a few myself? India was full of birds and animals, reptiles and insects, so why not put them into my stories?

And so I began writing animal stories—some true, some invented—and sending them out to magazines all over the world. And lo and behold, they were published!

My tiger cubs, pythons, panthers, hornbills, chameleons, baby elephants, monkeys, white mice, frogs, crows and crocodiles, all turned up in Australia (*The School Magazine*), the USA (*Highlights for Children* and *Cricket*), Scotland (*Blackwoods*), England (*The Lady*) and in most of our own Sunday supplements. Many got into anthologies and school readers, with the result that young readers often ask me, 'Sir did you really meet a leopard?' or 'Do you keep a python in the house?' or 'Sir, if you were chased by a bear you must be a fast runner.' And I have to scratch my head and make up a new story to justify the old one.

But my animals are real animals, and they behave as animals usually do. It's really the humans who do strange things. Animals are predictable. Humans, never.

Ruskin Bond

SECTION-I

To See a Tiger

Panther's Moon

1

IN THE entire village, he was the first to get up. Even the dog, a big hill mastiff called Sheroo, was asleep in a corner of the dark room, curled up near the cold embers of the previous night's fire. Bisnu's tousled head emerged from his blanket. He rubbed the sleep from his eyes and sat up on his haunches. Then, gathering his wits, he crawled in the direction of the loud ticking that came from the battered little clock which occupied the second-most honoured place in a niche in the wall. The most honoured place belonged to a picture of Ganesha, the god of learning, who had an elephant's head and a fat boy's body.

Bringing his face close to the clock, Bisnu could just make out the hands. It was five o'clock. He had half an hour in which to get ready and leave.

He got up, in vest and underpants, and moved quietly towards the door. The soft tread of his bare feet woke Sheroo, and the big black dog rose silently and padded behind the boy. The door opened and closed, and then the boy and the dog were outside in the early dawn. The month was June, and the nights were warm, even in the Himalayan valleys, but there was fresh dew on the grass. Bisnu felt the dew beneath his feet. He took a deep breath and began walking down to the stream.

The sound of the stream filled the small valley. At that early hour of the morning, it was the only sound, but Bisnu was hardly conscious of it. It was a sound he lived with and took for granted. It was only when he had crossed the hill, on his way to the town—and the sound of the stream grew distant—that he really began to notice it. And it was only when the stream was too far away to be heard that he really missed its sound.

He slipped out of his underclothes, gazed for a few moments at the goose pimples rising on his flesh, and then dashed into the shallow stream. As he went further in, the cold mountain water reached his loins and navel, and he gasped with shock and pleasure. He drifted slowly with the current, swam across to a small inlet which formed a fairly deep pool, and plunged into the water. Sheroo hated cold water at this early hour. Had the sun been up, he would not have hesitated to join Bisnu. Now he contented himself with sitting on a smooth rock and gazing placidly at the slim brown boy splashing about in the clear water in the widening light of dawn.

Bisnu did not stay long in the water. There wasn't time. When he returned to the house, he found his mother up, making tea and chapattis. His sister, Puja, was still asleep. She was a little older than Bisnu, a pretty girl with large black eyes, good teeth and strong arms and legs. During the day, she helped her mother in the house and in the fields. She did not go to the school with Bisnu. But when he came home in the evenings, he would try teaching her some of the things he had learnt. Their father was dead. Bisnu, at twelve, considered himself the head of the family.

He ate two chapattis, after spreading butter-oil on them. He drank a glass of hot sweet tea. His mother gave two thick chapattis to Sheroo, and the dog wolfed them down in a few minutes. Then she wrapped two chapattis and some gourd curry in some big green leaves, and handed these to Bisnu. This was his lunch packet. His mother and Puja would take their meal afterwards.

When Bisnu was dressed, he stood with folded hands before the picture of Ganesha. Ganesha is the god who blesses all beginnings. The author who begins to write a new book, the banker who opens a new ledger, the traveller who starts on a journey, all invoke the kindly help of Ganesha. And as Bisnu made a journey every day, he never left without the goodwill of the elephant-headed god.

How, one might ask, did Ganesha get his elephant's head?

When born, he was a beautiful child. Parvati, his mother, was so proud of him that she went about showing him to everyone. Unfortunately, she made the mistake of showing the child to that envious planet, Saturn, who promptly burnt off poor Ganesha's head. Parvati, in despair, went to Brahma, the Creator, for a new head for her son. He had no head to give her, but advised her to search for some man or animal caught in a sinful or wrong act. Parvati wandered about until she came upon an elephant sleeping with its head the wrong way, that is, to the south. She promptly removed the elephant's head and planted it on Ganesha's shoulders, where it took root.

Bisnu knew this story. He had heard it from his mother.

Wearing a white shirt and black shorts, and a pair of worn white keds, he was ready for his long walk to school, five miles up the mountain.

His sister woke up just as he was about to leave. She pushed the hair away from her face and gave Bisnu one of her rare smiles.

'I hope you have not forgotten,' she said.

'Forgotten?' said Bisnu, pretending innocence. 'Is there anything I am supposed to remember?'

'Don't tease me. You promised to buy me a pair of bangles, remember? I hope you won't spend the money on sweets, as you did last time.'

'Oh, yes, your bangles,' said Bisnu. 'Girls have nothing better to do than waste money on trinkets. Now, don't lose your temper! I'll get them for you. Red and gold are the colours you want?'

'Yes, Bhaiya,' said Puja gently, pleased that Bisnu had remembered the colours. 'And for your dinner tonight, we'll make you something special. Won't we, Mother?'

'Yes. But hurry up and get dressed. There is some ploughing to be done today. The rains will soon be here, if the gods are kind.'

'The monsoon will be late this year,' said Bisnu. 'Mr Nautiyal, our teacher, told us so. He said it had nothing to do with the gods.'

'Be off, you are getting late,' said Puja, before Bisnu could begin an argument with his mother. She was diligently winding the old clock. It was quite light in the room. The sun would be up any minute.

Bisnu shouldered his school bag, kissed his mother, pinched his sister's cheeks and left the house. He started climbing the steep path up the mountainside. Sheroo bounded ahead; for he, too, always went with Bisnu to school.

Five miles to school. Every day, except Sunday, Bisnu walked five miles to school; and in the evening, he walked home again. There was no school in his own small village of Manjari, for the village consisted of only five families. The nearest school was at Kemptee, a small township on the bus route through the district of Garhwal. A number of boys walked to school, from distances of two or three miles; their villages were not quite as remote as Manjari. But Bisnu's village lay right at the bottom of the mountain, a drop of over two thousand feet from Kemptee. There was no proper road between the village and the town.

In Kemptee there was a school, a small mission hospital, a post office and several shops. In Manjari village there were none of these amenities. If you were sick, you stayed at home until you got well; if you were very sick, you walked or were carried to the hospital, up the five-mile path. If you wanted to buy something, you went without it; but if you wanted it very badly, you could walk the five miles to Kemptee.

Manjari was known as the Five-Mile Village.

Twice a week, if there were any letters, a postman came to the village. Bisnu usually passed the postman on his way to and from school.

There were other boys in Manjari village, but Bisnu was the only one who went to school. His mother would not have fussed if he had stayed at home and worked in the fields. That was what the other boys did; all except lazy Chittru, who preferred fishing in the stream or helping himself to the fruit off other people's trees. But Bisnu went to school. He went because he wanted to. No one could force him to go; and no one could stop him from going. He had set his heart on receiving a good schooling. He wanted to read and write as well as anyone in the big world, the world that seemed to begin only where the mountains ended. He felt cut off from the world in his small valley. He would rather live at the top of a mountain than at the bottom of one. That was why he liked climbing to Kemptee, it took him to the top of the mountain; and from its ridge he could look down on his own valley to the north, and on the wide endless plains stretching towards the south.

The plainsman looks to the hills for the needs of his spirit but the hill man looks to the plains for a living.

Leaving the village and the fields below him, Bisnu climbed steadily up the bare hillside, now dry and brown. By the time the sun was up, he had entered the welcome shade of an oak and rhododendron forest. Sheroo went bounding ahead, chasing squirrels and barking at langurs.

A colony of langurs lived in the oak forest. They fed on oak leaves, acorns and other green things, and usually remained in the trees, coming down to the ground only to play or bask in the sun. They were beautiful, supple-limbed animals, with black faces and silver-grey coats and long, sensitive tails. They leapt from tree to tree with great agility. The young ones wrestled on the grass like boys.

A dignified community, the langurs did not have the cheekiness or dishonest habits of the red monkeys of the plains; they did not approach dogs or humans. But they had grown used to Bisnu's comings and goings, and did not fear him. Some of the older ones would watch him quietly, a little puzzled. They did not go near the town, because the Kemptee boys threw stones at them. And anyway, the oak forest gave them all the food they required.

Emerging from the trees, Bisnu crossed a small brook. Here he stopped to drink the fresh clean water of a spring. The brook tumbled down the mountain and joined the river a little below Bisnu's village. Coming from another direction was a second path, and at the junction of the two paths, Sarru was waiting for him.

Sarru came from a small village about three miles from Bisnu's and closer to the town. He had two large milk cans slung over his shoulders. Every morning he carried this milk to town, selling one can to the school and the other to Dr Taylor, the lady doctor at the small mission hospital. He was a little older than Bisnu but not as well-built.

They hailed each other, and Sarru fell into step beside Bisnu. They often met at this spot, keeping each other company for the remaining two miles to Kemptee.

'There was a panther in our village last night,' said Sarru.

This information interested but did not excite Bisnu. Panthers were common enough in the hills and did not usually present a problem except during the winter months, when their natural prey was scarce. Then, occasionally, a panther would take to haunting the outskirts of a village, seizing a careless dog or a stray goat.

'Did you lose any animals?' asked Bisnu.

'No. It tried to get into the cowshed but the dogs set up an alarm. We drove it off.'

'It must be the same one which came around last winter. We lost a calf and two dogs in our village.'

'Wasn't that the one the shikaris wounded? I hope it hasn't become a cattle lifter.'

'It could be the same. It has a bullet in its leg. These hunters are the people who cause all the trouble. They think it's easy to shoot a panther. It would be better if they missed altogether, but they usually wound it.'

'And then the panther's too slow to catch the barking deer, and starts on our own animals.'

'We're lucky it didn't become a man-eater. Do you remember the man-eater six years ago? I was very small then. My father told me all about it. Ten people were killed in our valley alone. What happened to it?'

'I don't know. Some say it poisoned itself when it ate the headman of another village.'

Bisnu laughed. 'No one liked that old villain. He must

have been a man-eater himself in some previous existence!' They linked arms and scrambled up the stony path. Sheroo began barking and ran ahead. Someone was coming down the path.

It was Mela Ram, the postman.

2

'Any letters for us?' asked Bisnu and Sarru together.

They never received any letters but that did not stop them from asking. It was one way of finding out who had received letters.

'You're welcome to all of them,' said Mela Ram. 'If you'll carry my bag for me.'

'Not today,' said Sarru. 'We're busy today. Is there a letter from Corporal Ghanshyam for his family?'

'Yes, there is a postcard for his people. He is posted on the Ladakh border now and finds it very cold there.'

Postcards, unlike sealed letters, were considered public property and were read by everyone. The senders knew that too, and so Corporal Ghanshyam Singh was careful to mention that he expected a promotion very soon. He wanted everyone in his village to know it.

Mela Ram, complaining of sore feet, continued on his way, and the boys carried on up the path. It was eight o'clock when they reached Kemptee. Dr Taylor's outpatients were just beginning to trickle in at the hospital gate. The doctor was trying to prop up a rose creeper which had blown down during the night. She liked attending to her plants in the mornings, before starting on her patients. She found this helped her in her work. There was a lot in common between ailing plants and ailing people.

Dr Taylor was fifty, white-haired but fresh in the face and

full of vitality. She had been in India for twenty years, and ten of these had been spent working in the hill regions.

She saw Bisnu coming down the road. She knew about the boy and his long walk to school and admired him for his keenness and sense of purpose. She wished there were more like him.

Bisnu greeted her shyly. Sheroo barked and put his paws up on the gate.

'Yes, there's a bone for you,' said Dr Taylor. She often put aside bones for the big black dog, for she knew that Bisnu's people could not afford to give the dog a regular diet of meat—though he did well enough on milk and chapattis.

She threw the bone over the gate and Sheroo caught it before it fell. The school bell began ringing and Bisnu broke into a run. Sheroo loped along behind the boy.

When Bisnu entered the school gate, Sheroo sat down on the grass of the compound. He would remain there until the lunch break. He knew of various ways of amusing himself during school hours and had friends among the bazaar dogs. But just then he didn't want company. He had his bone to get on with.

Mr Nautiyal, Bisnu's teacher, was in a bad mood. He was a keen rose grower and only that morning, on getting up and looking out of his bedroom window, he had been horrified to see a herd of goats in his garden. He had chased them down the road with a stick but the damage had already been done. His prize roses had all been consumed.

Mr Nautiyal had been so upset that he had gone without his breakfast. He had also cut himself whilst shaving. Thus, his mood had gone from bad to worse. Several times during the day, he brought down his ruler on the knuckles of any boy who irritated him. Bisnu was one of his best pupils. But even Bisnu irritated him by asking too many questions about a new sum which Mr Nautiyal didn't feel like explaining. That was the kind of day it was for Mr Nautiyal. Most schoolteachers know similar days.

'Poor Mr Nautiyal,' thought Bisnu. 'I wonder why he's so upset. It must be because of his pay. He doesn't get much money. But he's a good teacher. I hope he doesn't take another job.' But after Mr Nautiyal had eaten his lunch, his mood improved (as it always did after a meal), and the rest of the day passed serenely. Armed with a bundle of homework, Bisnu came out from the school compound at four o'clock, and was immediately joined by Sheroo. He proceeded down the road in the company of several of his classfellows. But he did not linger long in the bazaar. There were five miles to walk, and he did not like to get home too late. Usually, he reached his house just as it was beginning to get dark. Sarru had gone home long ago, and Bisnu had to make the return journey on his own. It was a good opportunity to memorize the words of an English poem he had been asked to learn.

Bisnu had reached the little brook when he remembered the bangles he had promised to buy for his sister.

'Oh, I've forgotten them again,' he said aloud. 'Now I'll catch it—and she's probably made something special for my dinner!'

Sheroo, to whom these words were addressed, paid no attention but bounded off into the oak forest. Bisnu looked around for the monkeys but they were nowhere to be seen.

'Strange,' he thought. 'I wonder why they have disappeared.' He was startled by a sudden sharp cry, followed by a fierce yelp. He knew at once that Sheroo was in trouble. The noise came from the bushes down the khud into which the dog had rushed but a few seconds previously.

Bisnu jumped off the path and ran down the slope towards

the bushes. There was no dog and not a sound. He whistled and called, but there was no response. Then he saw something lying on the dry grass. He picked it up. It was a portion of a dog's collar, stained with blood. It was Sheroo's collar and Sheroo's blood.

Bisnu did not search further. He knew, without a doubt, that Sheroo had been seized by a panther. No other animal could have attacked so silently and swiftly and carried off a big dog without a struggle. Sheroo was dead—must have been dead within seconds of being caught and flung into the air. Bisnu knew the danger that lay in wait for him if he followed the blood trail through the trees. The panther would attack anyone who interfered with its meal. With tears starting in his eyes, Bisnu carried on down the path to the village. His fingers still clutched the little bit of bloodstained collar that was all that was left of his dog.

3

Bisnu was not a very sentimental boy, but he sorrowed for his dog, who had been his companion on many a hike into the hills and forests. He did not sleep that night, but turned restlessly from side to side moaning softly. After some time he felt Puja's hand on his head. She began stroking his brow. He took her hand in his own and the clasp of her rough, warm, familiar hand gave him a feeling of comfort and security.

Next morning, when he went down to the stream to bathe, he missed the presence of his dog. He did not stay long in the water. It wasn't as much fun when there was no Sheroo to watch him.

When Bisnu's mother gave him his food, she told him to be careful and hurry home that evening. A panther, even if it is only a cowardly lifter of sheep or dogs, is not to be trifled with. And this particular panther had shown some daring by seizing the dog even before it was dark.

Still, there was no question of staying away from school. If Bisnu remained at home every time a panther put in an appearance, he might just as well stop going to school altogether.

He set off even earlier than usual and reached the meeting of the paths long before Sarru. He did not wait for his friend, because he did not feel like talking about the loss of his dog. It was not the day for the postman, and so Bisnu reached Kemptee without meeting anyone on the way. He tried creeping past the hospital gate unnoticed, but Dr Taylor saw him and the first thing she said was: 'Where's Sheroo? I've got something for him.'

When Dr Taylor saw the boy's face, she knew at once that something was wrong.

'What is it, Bisnu?' she asked. She looked quickly up and down the road. 'Is it Sheroo?'

He nodded gravely.

'A panther took him,' he said.

'In the village?'

'No, while we were walking home through the forest. I did not see anything—but I heard.'

Dr Taylor knew that there was nothing she could say that would console him, and she tried to conceal the bone which she had brought out for the dog, but Bisnu noticed her hiding it behind her back and the tears welled up in his eyes. He turned away and began running down the road.

His schoolfellows noticed Sheroo's absence and questioned Bisnu. He had to tell them everything. They were full of sympathy, but they were also quite thrilled at what had happened and kept pestering Bisnu for all the details. There was a lot of noise in the classroom, and Mr Nautiyal had to call for order.

When he learnt what had happened, he patted Bisnu on the head and told him that he need not attend school for the rest of the day. But Bisnu did not want to go home. After school, he got into a fight with one of the boys, and that helped him forget.

4

The panther that plunged the village into an atmosphere of gloom and terror may not have been the same panther that took Sheroo. There was no way of knowing, and it would have made no difference, because the panther that came by night and struck at the people of Manjari was that most feared of wild creatures—a man-eater.

Nine-year-old Sanjay, son of Kalam Singh, was the first child to be attacked by the panther.

Kalam Singh's house was the last in the village and nearest to the stream. Like the other houses, it was quite small, just a room above and a stable below, with steps leading up from outside the house. He lived there with his wife, two sons (Sanjay was the youngest) and little daughter Basanti, who had just turned three.

Sanjay had brought his father's cows home after grazing them on the hillside in the company of other children. He had also brought home an edible wild plant, which his mother cooked into a tasty dish for their evening meal. They had their food at dusk, sitting on the floor of their single room, and soon after, settled down for the night. Sanjay curled up in his favourite spot, with his head near the door, where he got a little fresh air. As the nights were warm, the door was usually left a little ajar. Sanjay's mother piled ash on the embers of the fire and the family was soon asleep.

No one heard the stealthy padding of a panther approaching

the door, pushing it wider open. But suddenly there were sounds of a frantic struggle, and Sanjay's stifled cries were mixed with the grunts of the panther. Kalam Singh leapt to his feet with a shout. The panther had dragged Sanjay out of the door and was pulling him down the steps, when Kalam Singh started battering at the animal with a large stone. The rest of the family screamed in terror, rousing the entire village. A number of men came to Kalam Singh's assistance, and the panther was driven off. But Sanjay lay unconscious.

Someone brought a lantern and the boy's mother screamed when she saw her small son with his head lying in a pool of blood. It looked as if the side of his head had been eaten off by the panther. But he was still alive, and as Kalam Singh plastered ash on the boy's head to stop the bleeding, he found that though the scalp had been torn off one side of the head, the bare bone was smooth and unbroken.

'He won't live through the night,' said a neighbour. 'We'll have to carry him down to the river in the morning.'

The dead were always cremated on the banks of a small river which flowed past Manjari village.

Suddenly the panther, still prowling about the village, called out in rage and frustration, and the villagers rushed to their homes in panic and barricaded themselves in for the night.

Sanjay's mother sat by the boy for the rest of the night, weeping and watching. Towards dawn he started to moan and show signs of coming round. At this sign of returning consciousness, Kalam Singh rose determinedly and looked around for his stick.

He told his elder son to remain with the mother and daughter, as he was going to take Sanjay to Dr Taylor at the hospital.

'See, he is moaning and in pain,' said Kalam Singh. 'That

means he has a chance to live if he can be treated at once.'

With a stout stick in his hand, and Sanjay on his back, Kalam Singh set off on the two miles of hard mountain track to the hospital at Kemptee. His son, a bloodstained cloth around his head, was moaning but still hadn't regained consciousness. When at last Kalam Singh climbed up through the last fields below the hospital, he asked for the doctor and stammered out an account of what had happened.

It was a terrible injury, as Dr Taylor discovered. The bone over almost one-third of the head was bare and the scalp was torn all round. As the father told his story, the doctor cleaned and dressed the wound, and then gave Sanjay a shot of penicillin to prevent sepsis. Later, Kalam Singh carried the boy home again.

5

After this, the panther went away for some time. But the people of Manjari could not be sure of its whereabouts. They kept to their houses after dark and shut their doors. Bisnu had to stop going to school, because there was no one to accompany him and it was dangerous to go alone. This worried him, because his final exam was only a few weeks off and he would be missing important classwork. When he wasn't in the fields, helping with the sowing of rice and maize, he would be sitting in the shade of a chestnut tree, going through his well-thumbed second-hand school books. He had no other reading, except for a copy of the Ramayana and a Hindi translation of *Alice in Wonderland*. These were well-preserved, read only in fits and starts, and usually kept locked in his mother's old tin trunk.

Sanjay had nightmares for several nights and woke up screaming. But with the resilience of youth, he quickly recovered. At the end of the week, he was able to walk to the hospital, though his father always accompanied him. Even a desperate panther will hesitate to attack a party of two. Sanjay, with his thin little face and huge bandaged head, looked a pathetic figure, but he was getting better and the wound looked healthy.

Bisnu often went to see him, and the two boys spent long hours together near the stream. Sometimes Chittru would join them, and they would try catching fish with a home-made net. They were often successful in taking home one or two mountain trout. Sometimes, Bisnu and Chittru wrestled in the shallow water or on the grassy banks of the stream. Chittru was a chubby boy with a broad chest, strong legs and thighs, and when he used his weight he got Bisnu under him. But Bisnu was hard and wiry and had very strong wrists and fingers. When he had Chittru in a vice, the bigger boy would cry out and give up the struggle. Sanjay could not join in these games. He had never been a very strong boy and he needed plenty of rest if his wounds were to heal well.

The panther had not been seen for over a week, and the people of Manjari were beginning to hope that it might have moved on over the mountain or further down the valley.

'I think I can start going to school again,' said Bisnu. 'The panther has gone away.'

'Don't be too sure,' said Puja. 'The moon is full these days and perhaps it is only being cautious.'

'Wait a few days,' said their mother. 'It is better to wait. Perhaps you could go the day after tomorrow when Sanjay goes to the hospital with his father. Then you will not be alone.'

And so, two days later, Bisnu went up to Kemptee with Sanjay and Kalam Singh. Sanjay's wound had almost healed over. Little islets of flesh had grown over the bone. Dr Taylor told him that he need come to see her only once a fortnight, instead of every third day.

Bisnu went to his school, and was given a warm welcome by his friends and by Mr Nautiyal.

'You'll have to work hard,' said his teacher. 'You have to catch up with the others. If you like, I can give you some extra time after classes.'

'Thank you, sir, but it will make me late,' said Bisnu. 'I must get home before it is dark, otherwise my mother will worry. I think the panther has gone but nothing is certain.'

'Well, you mustn't take risks. Do your best, Bisnu. Work hard and you'll soon catch up with your lessons.'

Sanjay and Kalam Singh were waiting for him outside the school. Together they took the path down to Manjari, passing the postman on the way. Mela Ram said he had heard that the panther was in another district and that there was nothing to fear. He was on his rounds again.

Nothing happened on the way. The langurs were back in their favourite part of the forest. Bisnu got home just as the kerosene lamp was being lit. Puja met him at the door with a winsome smile.

'Did you get the bangles?' she asked.

But Bisnu had forgotten again.

6

There had been a thunderstorm and some rain—a short, sharp shower which gave the villagers hope that the monsoon would arrive on time. It brought out the thunder lilies—pink, crocus-like flowers which sprang up on the hillsides immediately after a summer shower.

Bisnu, on his way home from school, was caught in the rain. He knew the shower would not last, so he took shelter in a small cave and, to pass the time, began doing sums, scratching figures in the damp earth with the end of a stick.

When the rain stopped, he came out from the cave and continued down the path. He wasn't in a hurry. The rain had made everything smell fresh and good. The scent from fallen pine needles rose from the wet earth. The leaves of the oak trees had been washed clean and a light breeze turned them about, showing their silver undersides. The birds, refreshed and high-spirited, set up a terrific noise. The worst offenders were the yellow-bottomed bulbuls who squabbled and fought in the blackberry bushes. A barbet, high up in the branches of a deodar, set up its querulous, plaintive call. And a flock of bright green parrots came swooping down the hill to settle in a wild plum tree and feast on the unripe fruit. The langurs, too, had been revived by the rain. They leapt friskily from tree to tree greeting Bisnu with little grunts.

He was almost out of the oak forest when he heard a faint bleating. Presently, a little goat came stumbling up the path towards him. The kid was far from home and must have strayed from the rest of the herd. But it was not yet conscious of being lost. It came to Bisnu with a hop, skip and a jump and started nuzzling against his legs like a cat.

'I wonder who you belong to,' mused Bisnu, stroking the little creature. 'You'd better come home with me until someone claims you.'

He didn't have to take the kid in his arms. It was used to humans and followed close at his heels. Now that darkness was coming on, Bisnu walked a little faster.

He had not gone very far when he heard the sawing grunt of a panther.

The sound came from the hill to the right, and Bisnu judged the distance to be anything from a hundred to two hundred yards. He hesitated on the path, wondering what to do. Then he picked the kid up in his arms and hurried on in the direction of home and safety.

The panther called again, much closer now. If it was an ordinary panther, it would go away on finding that the kid was with Bisnu. If it was the man-eater, it would not hesitate to attack the boy, for no man-eater fears a human. There was no time to lose and there did not seem much point in running. Bisnu looked up and down the hillside. The forest was far behind him and there were only a few trees in his vicinity. He chose a spruce.

The branches of the Himalayan spruce are very brittle and snap easily beneath a heavy weight. They were strong enough to support Bisnu's light frame. It was unlikely they would take the weight of a full-grown panther. At least that was what Bisnu hoped.

Holding the kid with one arm, Bisnu gripped a low branch and swung himself up into the tree. He was a good climber. Slowly but confidently he climbed half-way up the tree, until he was about twelve feet above the ground. He couldn't go any higher without risking a fall.

He had barely settled himself in the crook of a branch when the panther came into the open, running into the clearing at a brisk trot. This was no stealthy approach, no wary stalking of its prey. It was the man-eater, all right. Bisnu felt a cold shiver run down his spine. He felt a little sick.

The panther stood in the clearing with a slight thrusting forward of the head. This gave it the appearance of gazing intently and rather short-sightedly at some invisible object in the clearing. But there is nothing short-sighted about a panther's vision. Its sight and hearing are acute.

Bisnu remained motionless in the tree and sent up a prayer to all the gods he could think of. But the kid began bleating. The panther looked up and gave its deep-throated, rasping grunt—a fearsome sound, calculated to strike terror in any treeborne animal. Many a monkey, petrified by a panther's roar, has fallen from its perch to make a meal for Mr Spots. The man-eater was trying the same technique on Bisnu. But though the boy was trembling with fright, he clung firmly to the base of the spruce tree.

The panther did not make any attempt to leap up the tree. Perhaps it knew instinctively that this was not the type of tree that it could climb. Instead, it described a semicircle round the tree, keeping its face turned towards Bisnu. Then it disappeared into the bushes.

The man-eater was cunning. It hoped to put the boy off his guard, perhaps entice him down from the tree. For, a few seconds later, with a half-humorous growl, it rushed back into the clearing and then stopped, staring up at the boy in some surprise. The panther was getting frustrated. It snarled, and putting its forefeet up against the tree trunk began scratching at the bark in the manner of an ordinary domestic cat. The tree shook at each thud of the beast's paw.

Bisnu began shouting for help.

The moon had not yet come up. Down in Manjari village, Bisnu's mother and sister stood in their lighted doorway, gazing anxiously up the pathway. Every now and then, Puja would turn to take a look at the small clock.

Sanjay's father appeared in a field below. He had a kerosene lantern in his hand.

'Sister, isn't your boy home as yet?' he asked.

'No, he hasn't arrived. We are very worried. He should have been home an hour ago. Do you think the panther will be about tonight? There's going to be a moon.'

'True, but it will be dark for another hour. I will fetch the other menfolk, and we will go up the mountain for your boy. There may have been a landslide during the rain. Perhaps the path has been washed away.'

'Thank you, brother. But arm yourselves, just in case the panther is about.'

'I will take my spear,' said Kalam Singh. 'I have sworn to spear that devil when I find him. There is some evil spirit dwelling in the beast and it must be destroyed!'

'I am coming with you,' said Puja.

'No, you cannot go,' said her mother. 'It's bad enough that Bisnu is in danger. You stay at home with me. This is work for men.'

'I shall be safe with them,' insisted Puja. 'I am going, Mother!' And she jumped down the embankment into the field and followed Sanjay's father through the village.

Ten minutes later, two men armed with axes had joined Kalam Singh in the courtyard of his house, and the small party moved silently and swiftly up the mountain path. Puja walked in the middle of the group, holding the lantern. As soon as the village lights were hidden by a shoulder of the hill, the men began to shout—both to frighten the panther, if it was about, and to give themselves courage.

Bisnu's mother closed the front door and turned to the image of Ganesha, the god for comfort and help.

Bisnu's calls were carried on the wind, and Puja and the men heard him while they were still half a mile away. Their own shouts increased in volume and, hearing their voices, Bisnu felt strength return to his shaking limbs. Emboldened by the approach of his own people, he began shouting insults at the snarling panther, then throwing twigs and small branches at the enraged animal. The kid added its bleats to the boy's shouts, and the birds took up the chorus. The langurs squealed and grunted, and the searchers shouted themselves hoarse, and the panther howled with rage. The forest had never before been so noisy.

As the search party drew near, they could hear the panther's savage snarls, and hurried, fearing that perhaps Bisnu had been seized. Puja began to run.

'Don't rush ahead, girl,' said Kalam Singh. 'Stay between us.'

The panther, now aware of the approaching humans, stood still in the middle of the clearing, head thrust forward in a familiar stance. There seemed too many men for one panther. When the animal saw the light of the lantern dancing between the trees, it turned, snarled defiance and hate, and without another look at the boy in the tree, disappeared into the bushes. It was not yet ready for a showdown.

7

Nobody turned up to claim the little goat, so Bisnu kept it. A goat was a poor substitute for a dog, but, like Mary's lamb, it followed Bisnu wherever he went, and the boy couldn't help being touched by its devotion. He took it down to the stream, where it would skip about in the shallows and nibble the sweet grass that grew on the banks.

As for the panther, frustrated in its attempt on Bisnu's life, it did not wait long before attacking another human.

It was Chittru who came running down the path one afternoon, bubbling excitedly about the panther and the postman.

Chittru, deeming it safe to gather ripe bilberries in the daytime, had walked about half a mile up the path from the village, when he had stumbled across Mela Ram's mailbag lying on the ground. Of the postman himself there was no sign. But a trail of blood led through the bushes.

Once again, a party of men headed by Kalam Singh and accompanied by Bisnu and Chittru, went out to look for the postman. But though they found Mela Ram's bloodstained clothes, they could not find his body. The panther had made no mistake this time.

It was to be several weeks before Manjari had a new postman.

A few days after Mela Ram's disappearance, an old woman was sleeping with her head near the open door of her house. She had been advised to sleep inside with the door closed, but the nights were hot and anyway, the old woman was a little deaf, and in the middle of the night, an hour before moonrise, the panther seized her by the throat. Her strangled cry woke her grown-up son, and all the men in the village woke up at his shouts and came running.

The panther dragged the old woman out of the house and down the steps, but left her when the men approached with their axes and spears, and made off into the bushes. The old woman was still alive, and the men made a rough stretcher of bamboo and vines and started carrying her up the path. But they had not gone far when she began to cough, and because of her terrible throat wounds, her lungs collapsed and she died.

It was the 'dark of the month'—the week of the new moon when nights are darkest.

Bisnu, closing the front door and lighting the kerosene lantern, said, 'I wonder where that panther is tonight!'

The panther was busy in another village: Sarru's village.

A woman and her daughter had been out in the evening bedding the cattle down in the stable. The girl had gone into the house and the woman was following. As she bent down to go in at the low door, the panther sprang from the bushes. Fortunately, one of its paws hit the doorpost and broke the force of the attack, or the woman would have been killed.

When she cried out, the men came round shouting and the panther slunk off. The woman had deep scratches on her back and was badly shocked.

The next day, a small party of villagers presented themselves in front of the magistrate's office at Kemptee and demanded that something be done about the panther. But the magistrate was away on tour, and there was no one else in Kemptee who had a gun. Mr Nautiyal met the villagers and promised to write to a well-known shikari, but said that it would be at least a fortnight before the shikari would be able to come.

Bisnu was fretting because he could not go to school. Most boys would be only too happy to miss school, but when you are living in a remote village in the mountains and having an education is the only way of seeing the world, you look forward to going to school, even if it is five miles from home. Bisnu's exams were only two weeks off, and he didn't want to remain in the same class while the others were promoted. Besides, he knew he could pass even though he had missed a number of lessons. But he had to sit for the exams. He couldn't miss them.

'Cheer up, Bhaiya,' said Puja, as they sat drinking glasses of hot tea after their evening meal. 'The panther may go away once the rains break.'

'Even the rains are late this year,' said Bisnu. 'It's so hot and dry. Can't we open the door?'

'And be dragged down the steps by the panther?' said his mother. 'It isn't safe to have the window open, let alone the door.' And she went to the small window—through which a cat would have found difficulty in passing—and bolted it firmly.

With a sigh of resignation, Bisnu threw off all his clothes except his underwear and stretched himself out on the earthen floor.

'We will be rid of the beast soon,' said his mother. 'I know it in my heart. Our prayers will be heard, and you shall go to school and pass your exams.'

To cheer up her children, she told them a humorous story which had been handed down to her by her grandmother. It was all about a tiger, a panther, and a bear, the three of whom were made to feel very foolish by a thief hiding in the hollow trunk of a banyan tree. Bisnu was sleepy and did not listen very attentively. He dropped off to sleep before the story was finished.

When he woke, it was dark and his mother and sister were asleep on the cot. He wondered what it was that had woken him. He could hear his sister's easy breathing and the steady ticking of the clock. Far away an owl hooted—an unlucky sign, his mother would have said; but she was asleep and Bisnu was not superstitious.

And then he heard something scratching at the door, and the hair on his head felt tight and prickly. It was like a cat scratching, only louder. The door creaked a little whenever it felt the impact of the paw—a heavy paw, as Bisnu could tell from the dull sound it made.

'It's the panther,' he muttered under his breath, sitting up on the hard floor.

The door, he felt, was strong enough to resist the panther's weight. And if he set up an alarm, he could rouse the village. But the middle of the night was no time for the bravest of men to tackle a panther.

In a corner of the room stood a long bamboo stick with a sharp knife tied to one end, which Bisnu sometimes used for spearing fish. Crawling on all fours across the room, he grasped the home-made spear, and then, scrambling on to a cupboard, he drew level with the skylight window. He could get his head and shoulders through the window.

'What are you doing up there?' said Puja, who had woken

up at the sound of Bisnu shuffling about the room.

'Be quiet,' said Bisnu. 'You'll wake Mother.'

Their mother was awake by now. 'Come down from there, Bisnu. I can hear a noise outside.'

'Don't worry,' said Bisnu, who found himself looking down on the wriggling animal which was trying to get its paw in under the door. With his mother and Puja awake, there was no time to lose. He had got the spear through the window, and though he could not manoeuvre it so as to strike the panther's head, he brought the sharp end down with considerable force on the animal's rump.

With a roar of pain and rage, the man-eater leapt down from the steps and disappeared into the darkness. It did not pause to see what had struck it. Certain that no human could have come upon it in that fashion, it ran fearfully to its lair, howling until the pain subsided.

8

A panther is an enigma. There are occasions when it proves itself to be the most cunning animal under the sun, and yet the very next day, it will walk into an obvious trap that no self-respecting jackal would ever go near. One day a panther will prove itself to be a complete coward and run like a hare from a couple of dogs, and on the very next, it will dash in amongst half a dozen men sitting round a camp fire and inflict terrible injuries on them.

It is not often that a panther is taken by surprise, as its power of sight and hearing are very acute. It is a master at the art of camouflage, and its spotted coat is admirably suited for the purpose. It does not need heavy jungle to hide in. A couple of bushes and the light and shade from surrounding trees are enough to make it almost invisible.

Because the Manjari panther had been fooled by Bisnu, it did not mean that it was a stupid panther. It simply meant that it had been a little careless. And Bisnu and Puja, growing in confidence since their midnight encounter with the animal, became a little careless themselves.

Puja was hoeing the last field above the house and Bisnu, at the other end of the same field, was chopping up several branches of green oak, prior to leaving the wood to dry in the loft. It was late afternoon and the descending sun glinted in patches on the small river. It was a time of day when only the most desperate and daring of man-eaters would be likely to show itself.

Pausing for a moment to wipe the sweat from his brow, Bisnu glanced up at the hillside, and his eye caught sight of a rock on the brown of the hill which seemed unfamiliar to him. Just as he was about to look elsewhere, the round rock began to grow and then alter its shape, and Bisnu, watching in fascination, was at last able to make out the head and forequarters of the panther. It looked enormous from the angle at which he saw it, and for a moment he thought it was a tiger. But Bisnu knew instinctively that it was the man-eater.

Slowly, the wary beast pulled itself to its feet and began to walk round the side of the great rock. For a second it disappeared and Bisnu wondered if it had gone away. Then it reappeared and the boy was all excitement again. Very slowly and silently, the panther walked across the face of the rock until it was in direct line with the corner of the field where Puja was working.

With a thrill of horror Bisnu realized that the panther was stalking his sister. He shook himself free from the spell which had woven itself round him and shouting hoarsely, ran forward.

'Run, Puja, run!' he called. 'It's on the hill above you!'

Puja turned to see what Bisnu was shouting about. She saw him gesticulate to the hill behind her, looked up just in time to see the panther crouching for his spring.

With great presence of mind, she leapt down the banking of the field and tumbled into an irrigation ditch.

The springing panther missed its prey, lost its foothold on the slippery shale banking and somersaulted into the ditch a few feet away from Puja. Before the animal could recover from its surprise, Bisnu was dashing down the slope, swinging his axe and shouting, *'Maro, maro!'* (Kill, kill!)

Two men came running across the field. They, too, were armed with axes. Together with Bisnu they made a half-circle around the snarling animal, which turned at bay and plunged at them in order to get away. Puja wriggled along the ditch on her stomach. The men aimed their axes at the panther's head, and Bisnu had the satisfaction of getting in a well-aimed blow between the eyes. The animal then charged straight at one of the men, knocked him over and tried to get at his throat. Just then Sanjay's father arrived with his long spear. He plunged the end of the spear into the panther's neck.

The panther left its victim and ran into the bushes, dragging the spear through the grass and leaving a trail of blood on the ground. The men followed cautiously—all except the man who had been wounded and who lay on the ground, while Puja and the other womenfolk rushed up to help him.

The panther had made for the bed of the stream and Bisnu, Sanjay's father and their companion were able to follow it quite easily. The water was red where the panther had crossed the stream, and the rocks were stained with blood. After they had gone downstream for about a furlong, they found the panther lying still on its side at the edge of the water. It was mortally wounded, but it continued to wave its tail like an angry cat. Then, even the tail lay still.

'It is dead,' said Bisnu. 'It will not trouble us again in this body.'

'Let us be certain,' said Sanjay's father, and he bent down and pulled the panther's tail.

There was no response.

'It is dead,' said Kalam Singh. 'No panther would suffer such an insult were it alive!'

They cut down a long piece of thick bamboo and tied the panther to it by its feet. Then, with their enemy hanging upside down from the bamboo pole, they started back for the village.

'There will be a feast at my house tonight,' said Kalam Singh. 'Everyone in the village must come. And tomorrow we will visit all the villages in the valley and show them the dead panther, so that they may move about again without fear.'

'We can sell the skin in Kemptee,' said their companion. 'It will fetch a good price.'

'But the claws we will give to Bisnu,' said Kalam Singh, putting his arm around the boy's shoulders. 'He has done a man's work today. He deserves the claws.'

A panther's or tiger's claws are considered to be lucky charms.

'I will take only three claws,' said Bisnu. 'One each for my mother and sister, and one for myself. You may give the others to Sanjay and Chittru and the smaller children.'

As the sun set, a big fire was lit in the middle of the village of Manjari and the people gathered round it, singing and laughing. Kalam Singh killed his fattest goat and there was meat for everyone.

9

Bisnu was on his way home. He had just handed in his first paper, arithmetic, which he had found quite easy. Tomorrow it would be algebra, and when he got home he would have to practise square roots and cube roots and fractional coefficients.

Mr Nautiyal and the entire class had been happy that Bisnu had been able to sit for the exams. He was also a hero to them for his part in killing the panther. The story had spread through the villages with the rapidity of a forest fire, a fire which was now raging in Kemptee town.

When he walked past the hospital, he was whistling cheerfully. Dr Taylor waved to him from the veranda steps.

'How is Sanjay now?' she asked.

'He is well,' said Bisnu.

'And your mother and sister?'

'They are well,' said Bisnu.

'Are you going to get yourself a new dog?'

'I am thinking about it,' said Bisnu. 'At present I have a baby goat—I am teaching it to swim!'

He started down the path to the valley. Dark clouds had gathered and there was a rumble of thunder. A storm was imminent.

'Wait for me!' shouted Sarru, running down the path behind Bisnu, his milk cans clanging against each other. He fell into step beside Bisnu.

'Well, I hope we don't have any more man-eaters for some time,' he said. 'I've lost a lot of money by not being able to take milk up to Kemptee.'

'We should be safe as long as a shikari doesn't wound another panther. There was an old bullet wound in the man-eater's thigh. That's why it couldn't hunt in the forest. The deer were too fast for it.'

'Is there a new postman yet?'

'He starts tomorrow. A cousin of Mela Ram's.'

When they reached the parting of their ways, it had begun to rain a little.

'I must hurry,' said Sarru. 'It's going to get heavier any minute.'

'I feel like getting wet,' said Bisnu. 'This time it's the monsoon, I'm sure.'

Bisnu entered the forest on his own, and at the same time the rain came down in heavy opaque sheets. The trees shook in the wind, the langurs chattered with excitement.

It was still pouring when Bisnu emerged from the forest, drenched to the skin. But the rain stopped suddenly, just as the village of Manjari came in view. The sun appeared through a rift in the clouds. The leaves and the grass gave out a sweet, fresh smell.

Bisnu could see his mother and sister in the field transplanting the rice seedlings. The menfolk were driving the yoked oxen through the thin mud of the fields, while the children hung on to the oxen's tails, standing on the plain wooden harrows and, with weird cries and shouts, sending the animals almost at a gallop along the narrow terraces.

Bisnu felt the urge to be with them, working in the fields. He ran down the path, his feet falling softly on the wet earth. Puja saw him coming and waved to him. She met him at the edge of the field.

'How did you find your paper today?' she asked.

'Oh, it was easy.' Bisnu slipped his hand into hers and together they walked across the field. Puja felt something smooth and hard against her fingers, and before she could see what

Bisnu was doing, he had slipped a pair of bangles over her wrist.

'I remembered,' he said, with a sense of achievement.

Puja looked at the bangles and burst out: 'But they are blue, Bhaiya, and I wanted red and gold bangles!' And then, when she saw him looking crestfallen, she hurried on: 'But they are very pretty, and you did remember... Actually, they're just as nice as the red and gold bangles! Come into the house when you are ready. I have made something special for you.'

'I am coming,' said Bisnu, turning towards the house. 'You don't know how hungry a man gets, walking five miles to reach home!'

The Tiger in the Tunnel

Tembu, the boy, opened his eyes in the dark and wondered if his father was ready to leave the hut on his nightly errand. There was no moon that night, and the deathly stillness of the surrounding jungle was broken only occasionally by the shrill cry of a cicada. Sometimes from far off came the hollow hammering of a woodpecker, carried along on the faint breeze. Or the grunt of a wild boar could be heard as he dug up a favourite root. But these sounds were rare, and the silence of the forest always returned to swallow them up.

Baldeo, the watchman, was awake. He stretched himself, slowly unwinding the heavy shawl that covered him like a shroud. It was close on midnight and the chilly air made him shiver. The station, a small shack backed by heavy jungle, was a station only in name; for trains only stopped there, if at all, for a few seconds before entering the deep cutting that led to the tunnel. Most trains merely slowed down before taking the sharp curve before the cutting.

Baldeo was responsible for signalling whether or not the tunnel was clear of obstruction, and his hand-worked signal stood before the entrance. At night, it was his duty to see that the lamp was burning, and that the overland mail passed through safely.

'Shall I come too, Father?' asked Tembu sleepily, still lying huddled in a corner of the hut.

'No, it is cold tonight. Do not get up.'

Tembu, who was twelve, did not always sleep with his father at the station, for he also had to help in the home, where his mother and small sister were usually alone. They lived in a small tribal village on the outskirts of the forest, about three miles from the station. Their small rice fields did not provide them with more than a bare living, and Baldeo considered himself lucky to have got the job of khalasi at this small wayside signal-stop.

Still drowsy, Baldeo groped for his lamp in the darkness, then fumbled about in search of matches. When he had produced a light, he left the hut, closed the door behind him, and set off along the permanent way. Tembu had fallen asleep again.

Baldeo wondered whether the lamp on the signal post was still alight. Gathering his shawl closer about him, he stumbled on, sometimes along the rails, sometimes along the ballast. He longed to get back to his warm corner in the hut.

The eeriness of the place was increased by the neighbouring hills, which overhung the main line threateningly. On entering the cutting, with its sheer rock walls towering high above the rails, Baldeo could not help thinking about the wild animals he might encounter. He had heard many tales of the famous tunnel tiger, a man-eater who was supposed to frequent this spot; but he hardly believed these stories for, since his arrival at this place a month ago, he had not seen or even heard a tiger.

There had, of course, been panthers, and only a few days previously the villagers had killed one with their spears and axes. Baldeo had occasionally heard the sawing of a panther calling to its mate, but they had not come near the tunnel or shed.

Baldeo walked confidently for, being a tribal himself, he was used to the jungle and its ways. Like his forefathers, he carried a small axe, fragile to look at, but deadly when in use. With it, in three or four swift strokes, he could cut down a tree as neatly as if it had been sawn; and he prided himself on his skill in wielding it against wild animals. He had killed a young boar with it once, and the family had feasted on the flesh for three days. The axe-head of pure steel, thin but ringing true like a bell, had been made by his father over a charcoal fire. This axe was a part of himself, and wherever he went, be it to the local market seven miles away, or to a tribal dance, the axe was always in his hand. Occasionally, an official who had come to the station had offered him good money for the weapon; but Baldeo had no intention of parting with it.

The cutting curved sharply, and in the darkness, the black entrance to the tunnel loomed up menacingly. The signal light was out. Baldeo set to work to haul the lamp down by its chain. If the oil had finished, he would have to return to the hut for more. The mail train was due in five minutes.

Once more he fumbled for his matches. Then suddenly he stood still and listened. The frightened cry of a barking deer, followed by a crashing sound in the undergrowth, made Baldeo hurry. There was still a little oil in the lamp, and after an instant's hesitation he lit the lamp again and hoisted it back into position. Having done this, he walked quickly down the tunnel, swinging his own lamp, so that the shadows leapt up and down the soot-stained walls, and having made sure that the line was clear, he returned to the entrance and sat down to wait for the mail train.

The train was late. Sitting huddled up, almost dozing, he soon forgot his surroundings and began to nod off.

Back in the hut, the trembling of the ground told of the

approach of the train, and a low, distant rumble woke the boy, who sat up, rubbing the sleep from his eyes.

'Father, it's time to light the lamp,' he mumbled, and then, realizing that his father had been gone some time, he lay down again; but he was wide awake now, waiting for the train to pass, waiting for his father's returning footsteps.

A low grunt resounded from the top of the cutting. In a second Baldeo was awake, all his senses alert. Only a tiger could emit such a sound.

There was no shelter for Baldeo, but he grasped his axe firmly and tensed his body, trying to make out the direction from which the animal was approaching. For some time there was only silence, even the usual jungle noises seemed to have ceased altogether. Then a thump and the rattle of small stones announced that the tiger had sprung into the cutting.

Baldeo, listening as he had never listened before, wondered if it was making for the tunnel or the opposite direction— the direction of the hut, in which Tembu would be lying unprotected. He did not have to wonder for long. Before a minute had passed, he made out the huge body of the tiger trotting steadily towards him. Its eyes shone a brilliant green in the light from the signal lamp. Flight was useless, for in the dark, the tiger would be more sure-footed than Baldeo and would soon be upon him from behind. Baldeo stood with his back to the signal post, motionless, staring at the great brute moving rapidly towards him. The tiger, used to the ways of men, for it had been preying on them for years, came on fearlessly, and with a quick run and a snarl struck out with its right paw, expecting to bowl over this puny man who dared stand in the way.

Baldeo, however, was ready. With a marvellously agile leap he avoided the paw and brought his axe down on the animal's shoulder. The tiger gave a roar and attempted to close in. Again Baldeo drove his axe with true aim; but, to his horror, the beast swerved, and the axe caught the tiger on the shoulder, almost severing the leg. To make matters worse, the axe remained stuck in the bone, and Baldeo was left without a weapon.

The tiger, roaring with pain, now sprang upon Baldeo, bringing him down and then tearing at his broken body. It was all over in a few minutes. Baldeo was conscious only of a searing pain down his back, and then there was blackness and the night closed in on him forever.

The tiger drew off and sat down licking his wounded leg, roaring every now and then with agony. He did not notice the faint rumble that shook the earth, followed by the distant puffing of an engine steadily climbing. The overland mail was approaching. Through the trees beyond the cutting, as the train advanced, the glow of the furnace could be seen; and showers of sparks fell like Diwali lights over the forest.

As the train entered the cutting, the engine whistled once, loud and piercingly. The tiger raised his head, then slowly got to his feet. He found himself trapped like the man. Flight along the cutting was impossible. He entered the tunnel, running as fast as his wounded leg would carry him. And then, with a roar and a shower of sparks, the train entered the yawning tunnel. The noise in the confined space was deafening; but, when the train came out into the open, on the other side, silence returned once more to the forest and the tunnel.

At the next station, the driver slowed down and stopped his train to water the engine. He got down to stretch his legs and decided to examine the head-lamps. He received the surprise of his life; for, just above the cowcatcher lay the major portion of the tiger, cut in half by the engine.

There was considerable excitement and conjecture at the

station, but back at the cutting there was no sound except for the sobs of the boy as he sat beside the body of his father. He sat there a long time, unafraid of the darkness, guarding the body from jackals and hyenas, until the first faint light of dawn brought with it the arrival of the relief watchman.

Tembu and his sister and mother were plunged in grief for two whole days; but life had to go on, and a living had to be made, and all the responsibility now fell on Tembu. Three nights later, he was at the cutting, lighting the signal lamp for the overland mail.

He sat down in the darkness to wait for the train, and sang softly to himself. There was nothing to be afraid of—his father had killed the tiger, the forest gods were pleased; and besides, he had the axe with him, his father's axe, and he knew how to use it.

No Room for a Leopard

I FIRST SAW the leopard when I was crossing the small stream at the bottom of the hill. The ravine was so deep that for most of the day it remained in shadow. This encouraged many birds and animals to emerge from cover during the hours of daylight. Few people ever passed that way; only milkmen and charcoal burners from the surrounding villages. As a result, the ravine had become a little haven for wildlife, one of the few natural sanctuaries left near Mussoorie.

Below my cottage was a forest of oak and maple and Himalayan rhododendron. A narrow path twisted its way down through the trees, over an open ridge where red sorrel grew wild, and then down steeply through a tangle of wild raspberries, creeping vines and slender rangal bamboo. At the bottom of the hill, a path led onto a grassy verge surrounded by wild dogroses. The streams ran close by the verge, tumbling over smooth pebbles, over rock worn yellow with age, on its way to the plains and to the little Song River and finally to the sacred Ganga.

Nearly every morning, and sometimes during the day, I heard the cry of the barking deer. And in the evening, walking through the forest, I disturbed parties of kalij pheasants. The birds went gliding into the ravines on open, motionless wings. I saw pine martins and a handsome red fox. I recognized the footprints of a bear.

As I had not come to take anything from the jungle, the birds and animals soon grew accustomed to my face. Or possibly they recognized my footsteps. After some time, my approach did not disturb them. A spotted forktail, which at first used to fly away, now remained perched on a boulder in the middle of the stream while I got across by means of other boulders only a few yards away.

The langurs in the oak and rhododendron trees who would at first go leaping through the branches at my approach, now watched me with some curiosity as they munched on the tender green shoots of the oak. The young ones scuffled and wrestled like boys while their parents groomed each other's coats, stretching themselves out on the sunlit hillside—beautiful animals with slim waists and long sinewy legs and tails full of character. But one evening, as I passed, I heard them chattering in the trees and I was not the cause of their excitement.

As I crossed the stream and began climbing the hill, the grunting and chattering increased, as though the langurs were trying to warn me of some hidden danger. A shower of pebbles came rattling down the steep hillside and I looked up to see a sinewy orange-gold leopard, poised on a rock about twenty feet above me.

It was not looking towards me but had its head thrust attentively forward in the direction of the ravine. It must have sensed my presence because it slowly turned its head and looked down at me. It seemed a little puzzled at my presence there, and when, to give myself courage, I clapped my hands sharply, the leopard sprang away into the thickets, making absolutely no sound as it melted into the shadows. I had disturbed the animal in its quest for food. But a little later, I heard the quickening cry of a barking deer as it fled through the forest—the hunt was still on.

The leopard, like other members of the cat family, is nearing extinction in India and I was surprised to find one so close to Mussoorie. Probably the deforestation that had been taking place in the surrounding hills had driven the deer into this green valley and the leopard, naturally, had followed.

It was some weeks before I saw the leopard again although I was often made aware of its presence. A dry rasping cough sometimes gave it away. At times I felt certain that I was being followed. And once, when I was late getting home, I was startled by a family of porcupines running about in a clearing. I looked around nervously and saw two bright eyes staring at me from a thicket. I stood still, my heart banging away against my ribs. Then the eyes danced away and I realized they were only fireflies.

In May and June, when the hills were brown and dry, it was always cool and green near the stream where ferns, maidenhair, and long grasses continued to thrive.

One day I found the remains of a barking deer that had been partially eaten. I wondered why the leopard had not hidden the remains of his meal and decided that he had been disturbed while eating. Then climbing the hill, I met a party of shikaris resting beneath the oaks. They asked me if I had seen a leopard. I said I had not. They said they knew there was a leopard in the forest. Leopard skins, they told me, were selling in Delhi at over a thousand rupees each! Of course there was a ban on the export of its skins but they gave me to understand that there were ways and means... I thanked them for their information and moved on, feeling uneasy and disturbed.

The shikaris had seen the carcass of the deer and the leopard's pug marks and they kept coming to the forest. Almost every evening I heard their guns banging away, for they were ready to fire at almost everything.

'There's a leopard about,' they told me. 'You should carry a gun.'

'I don't have one,' I said.

There were fewer birds to be seen and even the langurs had moved on. The red fox did not show itself and the pine martens who had earlier become bold, now dashed into hiding at my approach. The smell of one human is like the smell of any other.

I thought no more of the men. My attitude towards them was similar to the attitude of the denizens of the forest—they were men, unpredictable and to be avoided if possible.

One day after crossing the stream, I climbed Pari Tibba, a bleak, scrub-covered hill where no one lived. This was a stiff undertaking, because there was no path to the top and I had to scramble up a precipitous rock-face with the help of rocks and roots which were apt to come away in my groping hand. But at the top was a plateau with a few pine trees, their upper branches catching the wind and humming softly. There I found the ruins of what must have been the first settlers—just a few piles of rubble now overgrown with weeds, sorrel, dandelion and nettles.

As I walked through the roofless ruins, I was struck by the silence that surrounded me, the absence of birds and animals, the sense of complete desolation. The silence was so absolute that it seemed to be shouting in my ears. But there was something else of which I was becoming increasingly aware—the strong feline odour of one of the cat family. I paused and looked about. I was alone. There was no movement of dry leaf or loose stone. The ruins were, for the most part, open to the sky.

Their rotting rafters had collapsed and joined together to form a low passage, like the entrance to a mine. This dark cavern seemed to lead down.

The smell was stronger when I approached this spot so I stopped again and waited there, wondering if I had discovered the lair of the leopard, wondering if the animal was now at rest after a night's hunt. Perhaps it was crouched there in the dark, watching me, recognizing me, knowing me as a man who walked alone in the forest without a weapon. I like to think that he was there and that he knew me and that he acknowledged my visit in the friendliest way—by ignoring me altogether.

Perhaps I had made him confident—too confident, too careless, too trusting of the human in his midst. I did not venture any further. I did not seek physical contact or even another glimpse of that beautiful sinewy body, springing from rock to rock... It was his trust I wanted and I think he gave it to me. But did the leopard, trusting one man, make the mistake of bestowing his trust on others? Did I, by casting out all fear—my own fear and the leopard's protective fear—leave him defenceless?

Because next day, coming up the path from the stream, shouting and beating their drums, were the shikaris. They had a long bamboo pole across their shoulder and slung from the pole, feet up, head down, was the lifeless body of the leopard. It had been shot in the neck and in the head.

'We told you there was a leopard!' they shouted, in great good humour. 'Isn't he a fine specimen?'

'Yes,' I said. 'He was a beautiful leopard.'

I walked home through the silent forest. It was very silent, almost as though the birds and animals knew their trust had been violated.

I remembered the lines of a poem by D.H. Lawrence and

as I climbed the steep and lonely path to my home, the words beat out their rhythm in my mind—'There was room in the world for a mountain lion and me.'

A Tiger in the House

Tᴎᴏᴛʜʏ, ᴛʜᴇ tiger cub, was discovered by Grandfather on a hunting expedition in the Terai jungle near Dehra.

Grandfather was no shikari, but as he knew the forests of the Siwalik hills better than most people, he was persuaded to accompany the party—it consisted of several Very Important Persons from Delhi—to advise on the terrain and the direction the beaters should take once a tiger had been spotted.

The camp itself was sumptuous—seven large tents (one for each shikari), a dining tent and a number of servants' tents. The dinner was very good—as Grandfather admitted afterwards, it was not often that one saw hot-water plates, finger glasses and seven or eight courses in a tent in the jungle! But that was how things were done in the days of the Viceroys... There were also some fifteen elephants, four of them with howdahs for the shikaris, and the others specially trained for taking part in the beat.

The sportsmen never saw a tiger, nor did they shoot anything else, though they saw a number of deer, peacock and wild boar. They were giving up all hope of finding a tiger and were beginning to shoot at jackals, when Grandfather, strolling down the forest path at some distance from the rest of the party, discovered a little tiger about eighteen inches long, hiding among the intricate roots of a banyan tree. Grandfather picked him up and brought him home after the camp had broken up. He had the distinction of being the only member of the party to have bagged any game, dead or alive.

At first the tiger cub, who was named Timothy by Grandmother, was brought up entirely on milk given to him in a feeding bottle by our cook, Mehmoud. But the milk proved too rich for him, and he was put on a diet of raw mutton and cod liver oil, to be followed later by a more tempting diet of pigeons and rabbits.

Timothy was provided with two companions—Toto the monkey, who was bold enough to pull the young tiger by the tail, and then climb up the curtains if Timothy lost his temper; and a small mongrel puppy, found on the road by Grandfather.

At first, Timothy appeared to be quite afraid of the puppy and darted back with a spring if it came too near. He would make absurd dashes at it with his large forepaws and then retreat to a ridiculously safe distance. Finally, he allowed the puppy to crawl on his back and rest there!

One of Timothy's favourite amusements was to stalk anyone who would play with him, and so, when I came to live with Grandfather, I became one of the tiger's favourites. With a crafty look in his glittering eyes, and his body crouching, he would creep closer and closer to me, suddenly making a dash for my feet, rolling over on his back and kicking with delight, and pretending to bite my ankles.

He was by this time the size of a full-grown retriever, and when I took him out for walks, people on the road would give us a wide berth. When he pulled hard on his chain, I had difficulty in keeping up with him. His favourite place in the house was the drawing room, and he would make himself comfortable on the long sofa, reclining there with great dignity and snarling at anybody who tried to get him off.

Timothy had clean habits, and would scrub his face with his paws exactly like a cat. He slept at night in the cook's quarters, and was always delighted at being let out by him in the morning.

'One of these days,' declared Grandmother in her prophetic manner, 'we are going to find Timothy sitting on Mehmoud's bed, and no sign of the cook except his clothes and shoes!'

Of course, it never came to that, but when Timothy was about six months old, a change came over him; he grew steadily less friendly. When out for a walk with me, he would try to steal away to stalk a cat or someone's pet Pekinese. Sometimes at night we would hear frenzied cackling from the poultry house, and in the morning there would be feathers lying all over the veranda. Timothy had to be chained up more often. And, finally, when he began to stalk Mehmoud about the house with what looked like villainous intent, Grandfather decided it was time to transfer him to a zoo.

The nearest zoo was at Lucknow, two hundred miles away.

Reserving a first-class compartment for himself and Timothy—no one would share a compartment with them—Grandfather took him to Lucknow where the zoo authorities were only too glad to receive as a gift a well-fed and fairly civilized tiger.

About six months later, when my grandparents were visiting relatives in Lucknow, Grandfather took the opportunity of calling at the zoo to see how Timothy was getting on. I was not there to accompany him, but I heard all about it when he returned to Dehra.

Arriving at the zoo, Grandfather made straight for the

particular cage in which Timothy had been interned. The tiger was there, crouched in a corner, full-grown and with a magnificent striped coat.

'Hello, Timothy!' said Grandfather and, climbing the railing with ease, he put his arm through the bars of the cage.

The tiger approached the bars and allowed Grandfather to put both hands around his head. Grandfather stroked the tiger's forehead and tickled his ear, and, whenever he growled, smacked him across the mouth, which was his old way of keeping him quiet.

He licked Grandfather's hands and only sprang away when a leopard in the next cage snarled at him. Grandfather 'shooed' the leopard away and the tiger returned to lick his hands; but every now and then the leopard would rush at the bars and the tiger would slink back to his corner.

A number of people had gathered to watch the reunion when a keeper pushed his way through the crowd and asked Grandfather what he was doing.

'I'm talking to Timothy,' said Grandfather. 'Weren't you here when I gave him to the zoo six months ago?'

'I haven't been here very long,' said the surprised keeper. 'Please continue your conversation. But I have never been able to touch him myself, he is always very bad-tempered.'

'Why don't you put him somewhere else?' suggested Grandfather. 'That leopard keeps frightening him. I'll go and see the superintendent about it.'

Grandfather went in search of the superintendent of the zoo, but found that he had gone home early; and so, after wandering about the zoo for a little while, he returned to Timothy's cage to say goodbye. It was beginning to get dark.

He had been stroking and slapping Timothy for about five minutes when he found another keeper observing him with some alarm. Grandfather recognized him as the keeper who had been there when Timothy had first come to the zoo.

'*You* remember me,' said Grandfather. 'Now why don't you transfer Timothy to another cage, away from this stupid leopard?'

'But—sir—' stammered the keeper, 'it is not your tiger.'

'I know, I know,' said Grandfather testily. 'I realize he is no longer mine. But you might at least take a suggestion or two from me.'

'I remember your tiger very well,' said the keeper. 'He died two months ago.'

'Died!' exclaimed Grandfather.

'Yes, sir, of pneumonia. This tiger was trapped in the hills only last month, and he is very dangerous!'

Grandfather could think of nothing to say. The tiger was still licking his arm, with increasing relish. Grandfather took what seemed to him an age to withdraw his hand from the cage.

With his face near the tiger's he mumbled, 'Goodnight, Timothy,' and giving the keeper a scornful look, walked briskly out of the zoo.

To See a Tiger

M<small>R</small> K<small>ISHORE</small> drove me out to the forest rest house in his jeep, told me he'd be back in two days, and left me in the jungle. The caretaker of the rest house, a retired Indian Army corporal, made me a cup of tea.

'You have come to see the animals, sir?'

'Yes,' I said, looking around the clearing in front of the house, where a few domestic fowls scrabbled in the dust. 'Will I have to go far?'

'This is the best place, sir,' said the caretaker. 'See, the river is just below.'

A stream of clear mountain water ran through a shady glade of sal and sheesham trees about fifty yards from the house.

'The animals come at night,' said the caretaker. 'You can sit in the veranda with a cup of tea, and watch them. You must be very quiet, of course.'

'Will I see a tiger?' I asked. 'I've *come* to see a tiger.'

'Perhaps the tiger will come, sir,' said the caretaker with a tolerant smile. 'He will do his best, I am sure.'

He made me a simple lunch of rice and lentils, flavoured with a mango pickle. I spent the afternoon with a book taken from the rest house bookshelf. The small library hadn't been touched for over twenty years, and I had to make my choice from Marie Corelli, P.C. Wren, and early Wodehouse. I plumped for a Wodehouse—*Love Among the Chickens.* A peacock flaunted its tail feathers on the lawn, but I was not distracted. I had seen plenty of peacocks.

When it grew dark, I took up my position in the veranda, on an old cane chair. Bhag Singh, the caretaker, brought me dinner on a brass thali, with two different vegetables in separate katoris. The chapattis came in relays, brought hot from the kitchen by Bhag Singh's ten-year-old son. Then, sustained by more tea, sweet and milky, I began my vigil. It took an hour for Bhag Singh's family to settle down for the night in their outhouse. Their pi-dog stood outside, barking at me for half an hour, before he, too, fell asleep. The moon came up over the foothills, and the stream could be seen quite clearly.

And then a strange sound filled the night air. Not the roar of a tiger, nor the sawing of a leopard, but a rising crescendo of noise—wurk, wurk, wurk—issuing from the muddy banks near the stream. All the frogs in the jungle seemed to have gathered there that night. They must have been having a sort of Old Boys' Reunion, because everyone seemed to have something to say for himself. The speeches continued for about an hour. Then the meeting broke up, and silence returned to the forest.

A jackal slunk across the clearing. A puff of wind brushed through the trees. I was almost asleep when a cicada burst into violent music in a nearby tree. I started, and stared out at the silver, moon-green stream; but no animals came to drink that night. The next evening, Bhag Singh offered to sit up with me. He placed a charcoal burner on the veranda, and topped it with a large basin of tea.

'Whenever you feel sleepy, sir, I'll give you a glass of tea.'

Did we hear a panther—or was it someone sawing wood? The sounds are similar, in the distance. The frogs started up again. The Old Boys must have brought their wives along this time, because instead of speeches there was general conversation, exactly like the natter of a cocktail party.

By morning I had drunk over fifteen cups of tea. Out of respect for my grandfather, a pioneer tea planter in India, I did not complain. Bhag Singh made me an English breakfast—toast, fried eggs and more tea.

The third night passed in much the same way, except that Bhag Singh's son stayed up with us and drank his quota of tea.

In the morning, Mr Kishore came for me in his jeep.

'Did you see anything?'

'A jackal,' I said.

'Never mind, you'll have better luck next time. Of course, the jungles aren't what they used to be.'

I said goodbye to Bhag Singh, and got into the jeep.

We had gone barely a hundred yards along the forest road when Mr Kishore brought the jeep to a sudden, jolting halt.

Right in the middle of the road, about thirty yards in front of us, stood a magnificent full-grown tiger.

The tiger didn't roar. He didn't even snarl. But he gave us what appeared to be a quick, disdainful glance, and then walked majestically across the road and into the jungle.

'What luck!' exclaimed Mr Kishore. 'You can't complain now, can you? You've seen your tiger!'

'Yes,' I said. 'Three sleepless nights, and I've seen it in broad daylight!'

'Never mind,' said Mr Kishore. 'If you're tired, I know just the thing for you—a nice cup of tea.'

I think it was Malcolm Muggeridge who said that the only real Englishmen left in the world were to be found in India.

Tiger, Tiger, Burning Bright

O<small>N THE</small> left bank of the Ganga, where it emerges from the Himalayan foothills, there is a long stretch of heavy forest. These are villages on the fringe of the forest, inhabited by bamboo cutters and farmers, but there are few signs of commerce or pilgrimage. Hunters, however, have found the area an ideal hunting ground during the last seventy years, and, as a result, the animals are not as numerous as they used to be. The trees, too, have been disappearing slowly; and, as the forest recedes, the animals lose their food and shelter and move on further into the foothills. Slowly, they are being denied the right to live.

Only the elephant can cross the river. And two years ago, when a large area of the forest was cleared to make way for a refugee resettlement camp, a herd of elephants—finding their favourite food, the green shoots of the bamboo, in short supply—waded across the river. They crashed through the suburbs of Haridwar, knocked down a factory wall, pulled down several tin roofs, held up a train, and left a trail of devastation in their wake until they found a new home in a new forest which was still untouched. Here, they settled down to a new life—but an unsettled, wary life. They did not know when men would appear again, with tractors, bulldozers, and dynamite.

There was a time when the forest on the banks of the Ganga had provided food and shelter for some thirty or forty tigers; but men in search of trophies had shot them all, and now there remained only one old tiger in the jungle. Many hunters had tried to get him, but he was a wise and crafty old tiger, who knew the ways of men, and he had so far survived all attempts on his life.

Although the tiger had passed the prime of his life, he had lost none of his majesty. His muscles rippled beneath the golden yellow of his coat, and he walked through the long grass with the confidence of one who knew that he was still a king, even though his subjects were fewer. His great head pushed through the foliage, and it was only his tail, swinging high, that showed occasionally above the sea of grass.

In late spring he would head for the large jheel, the only water in the forest (if you don't count the river, which was several miles away), which was almost a lake during the rainy season, but just a muddy marsh at this time of the year.

Here, at different times of the day and night, all the animals came to drink—the long-horned sambhar, the delicate chital, the swamp deer, the hyenas and jackals, the wild boar, the panthers—and the lone tiger. Since the elephants had gone, the water was usually clear except when buffaloes from the nearest village came to wallow in it, and then it was very muddy. These buffaloes, though they were not wild, were not afraid of the panther or even of the tiger. They knew the panther was afraid of their massive horns and that the tiger preferred the flesh of the deer.

One day, there were several sambhars at the water's edge; but they did not stay long. The scent of the tiger came with the breeze, and there was no mistaking its strong feline odour. The deer held their heads high for a few moments, their nostrils twitching, and then scattered into the forest, disappearing behind a screen of leaf and bamboo.

When the tiger arrived, there was no other animal near the water. But the birds were still there. The egrets continued to wade in the shallows, and a kingfisher darted low over the water, dived suddenly—a flash of blue and gold—and made off with a slim silver fish, which glistened in the sun like a polished gem. A long brown snake glided in and out among the waterlilies and disappeared beneath a fallen tree which lay rotting in the shallows.

The tiger waited in the shelter of a rock, his ears pricked up for the least unfamiliar sound; he knew that it was at that place that men sometimes sat up for him with guns, for they coveted his beauty—his stripes, and the gold of his body, his fine teeth, his whiskers and his noble head. They would have liked to hang his skin on a wall, with his head stuffed and mounted, and pieces of glass replacing his fierce eyes. Then they would have boasted of their triumph over the king of the jungle.

The tiger had encountered hunters before, so he did not usually show himself in the open during the day. But of late he had heard no guns, and if there were hunters around, you would have heard their guns (for a man with a gun cannot resist letting it off, even if it is only at a rabbit—or at another man). And, besides, the tiger was thirsty.

He was also feeling quite hot. It was March, and the shimmering dust haze of summer had come early. Tigers—unlike other cats—are fond of water, and on a hot day will wallow in it for hours.

He walked into the water, in amongst the waterlilies, and drank slowly. He was seldom in a hurry when he ate or drank.

Other animals might bolt down their food, but they are only other animals. A tiger is a tiger; he has his dignity to preserve even though he isn't aware of it!

He raised his head and listened, one paw suspended in the air. A strange sound had come to him on the breeze, and he was wary of strange sounds. So he moved swiftly into the shelter of the tall grass that bordered the jheel, and climbed a hillock until he reached his favourite rock. This rock was big enough both to hide him and to give him shade. Anyone looking up from the jheel would have thought it strange that the rock had a round bump on the top. The bump was the tiger's head. He kept it very still.

The sound he heard was only the sound of a flute, rendered thin and reedy in the forest. It belonged to Ramu, a slim brown boy who rode a buffalo. Ramu played vigorously on the flute. Shyam, a slightly smaller boy, riding another buffalo, brought up the rear of the herd.

There were about eight buffaloes in the herd, and they belonged to the families of the two friends Ramu and Shyam. Their people were Gujars, a nomadic community who earned a livelihood by keeping buffaloes and selling milk and butter. The boys were about twelve years old, but they could not have told you exactly, because in their village nobody thought birthdays were important. They were almost the same age as the tiger, but he was old and experienced while they were still cubs.

The tiger had often seen them at the jheel, and he was not worried by their presence. He knew the village people would do him no harm as long as he left their buffaloes alone. Once, when he was younger and full of bravado, he had killed a buffalo—not because he was hungry, but because he was young and wanted to try out his strength—and after that the villagers had hunted him for days, with spears, bows and an old muzzleloader. Now he left the buffaloes alone, even though the deer in the forest were not as numerous as before.

The boys knew that a tiger lived in the jungle, for they had often heard him roar; but they did not suspect that he was so near just then.

The tiger gazed down from his rock, and the sight of eight fat black buffaloes made him give a low, throaty moan. But the boys were there. Besides, a buffalo was not easy to kill.

He decided to move on and find a cool shady place in the heart of the jungle where he could rest during the warm afternoon and be free of the flies and mosquitoes that swarmed around the jheel. At night he would hunt.

With a lazy, half-humorous roar—'*A-oonh!*'—he got up off his haunches and sauntered off into the jungle.

Even the gentlest of the tiger's roars can be heard half a mile away, and the boys, who were barely fifty yards away, looked up immediately.

'There he goes!' said Ramu, taking the flute from his lips and pointing it towards the hillocks. He was not afraid, for he knew that this tiger was not interested in humans. 'Did you see him?'

'I saw his tail, just before he disappeared. He's a big tiger!'

'Do not call him tiger. Call him uncle, or maharaja.'

'Oh, why?'

'Don't you know that it's unlucky to call a tiger a tiger? My father always told me so. If you meet a tiger, and call him uncle, he will leave you alone.'

'I'll try and remember that,' said Shyam.

The buffaloes were now well inside the water, and some of them were lying down in the mud. Buffaloes love soft wet mud and will wallow in it for hours. The slushier the mud the better. Ramu, to avoid being dragged down into the mud with his buffalo, slipped off its back and plunged into the water. He waded to a small islet covered with reeds and waterlilies. Shyam was close behind him.

They lay down on their hard flat stomachs, on a patch of grass, and allowed the warm sun to beat down on their bare brown bodies.

Ramu was the more knowledgeable boy because he had been to Hardiwar and Dehradun several times with his father. Shyam had never been out of the village.

Shyam said, 'The pool is not so deep this year.'

'We have had no rain since January,' said Ramu. 'If we do not get rain soon the jheel may dry up altogether.'

'And then what will we do?'

'We? I don't know. There is a well in the village. But even that may dry up. My father told me that it did once, just about the time I was born, and everyone had to walk ten miles to the river for water.'

'And what about the animals?'

'Some will stay here and die. Others will go to the river. But there are too many people near the river now—and temples, houses and factories—so the animals stay away. And the trees have been cut, so that between the jungle and the river there is no place to hide. Animals are afraid of the open—they are afraid of men with guns.'

'Even at night?'

'At night men come in jeeps, with searchlights. They kill the deer for meat, and sell the skins of tigers and panthers.'

'I didn't know a tiger's skin was worth anything.'

'It's worth more than our skins,' said Ramu knowingly. 'It will fetch six hundred rupees. Who would pay that much for one of us?'

'Our fathers would.'

'True—if they had the money.'

'If my father sold his fields, he would get more than six hundred rupees.'

'True—but if he sold his fields, none of you would have anything to eat. A man needs land as much as a tiger needs a jungle.'

'Yes,' said Shyam. 'And that reminds me—my mother asked me to take some roots home.'

'I will help you.'

They walked deeper into the jheel until the water was up to their waists, and began pulling up waterlilies by the roots. The flower is beautiful, but the villagers value the root more. When it is cooked, it makes a delicious and nourishing dish. The plant multiples rapidly and is aways in good supply. In the year when famine hit the village, it was only the root of the waterlily that saved many from starvation.

When Shyam and Ramu had finished gathering roots, they emerged from the water and passed the time wrestling with each other, slipping about in the soft mud, which soon covered them from head to toe.

To get rid of the mud, they dived into the water again and swam across to their buffaloes. Then, jumping on to their backs and digging their heels into the thick hides, the boys raced them across the jheel, shouting and hollering so much that all the birds flew away in fright, and the monkeys set up a shrill chattering of their own in the dhak trees. In March, the flame of the forest, or dhak trees, are ablaze with bright scarlet and orange flowers.

It was evening, and the twilight was fading fast, when the buffalo herd finally wandered its way homeward, to be greeted outside the village by the barking of dogs, the gurgle of hookah pipes, and the homely smell of cow-dung smoke.

The tiger made a kill that night—a chital. He made his approach against the wind so that the unsuspecting spotted deer did not see him until it was too late. A blow on the deer's haunches from the tiger's paw brought it down, and then the great beast fastened his fangs on the deer's throat. It was all over in a few minutes. The tiger was too quick and strong, and the deer did not struggle much.

It was a violent end for so gentle a creature. But you must not imagine that in the jungle the deer live in permanent fear of death. It is only man, with his imagination and his fear of the hereafter, who is afraid of dying. In the jungle it is different. Sudden death appears at intervals. Wild creatures do not have to think about it, and so the sudden killing of one of their number by some predator of the forest is only a fleeting incident soon forgotten by the survivors.

The tiger feasted well, growling with pleasure as he ate his way up the body, leaving the entrails. When he had had his night's fill, he left the carcass for the vultures and jackals. The cunning old tiger never returned to the same carcass, even if there was still plenty left to eat. In the past, when he had gone back to a kill, he had often found a man sitting in a tree waiting for him with a rifle.

His belly filled, the tiger sauntered over to the edge of the forest and looked out across the sandy wasteland and the deep, singing river, at the twinkling lights of Rishikesh on the opposite bank, and raised his head and roared his defiance at mankind.

He was a lonesome bachelor. It was five or six years since he had a mate. She had been shot by the trophy hunters, and her two cubs had been trapped by men who do trade in wild animals. One went to a circus, where he had to learn tricks to amuse men and respond to the crack of a whip; the other, more fortunate, went first to a zoo in Delhi and was later transferred to a zoo in America.

Sometimes, when the old tiger was very lonely, he gave a great roar, which could be heard throughout the forest. The villagers thought he was roaring in anger, but the jungle knew that he was really roaring out of loneliness. When the sound of his roar had died away, he paused, standing still, waiting for an answering roar; but it never came. It was taken up instead by the shrill scream of a barbet high up in a sal tree.

It was dawn now, dew-fresh and cool, and the jungle dwellers were on the move. The black beady little eyes of a jungle rat were fixed on a brown hen who was pecking around in the undergrowth near her nest. He had a large family to feed, this rat, and he knew that in the hen's nest was a clutch of delicious fawn-coloured eggs. He waited patiently for nearly an hour before he had the satisfaction of seeing the hen leave her nest and go off in search of food.

As soon as she had gone, the rat lost no time in making his raid. Slipping quietly out of his hole, he slithered along among the leaves; but, clever as he was, he did not realize that his own movements were being watched.

A pair of grey mongooses scouted about in the dry grass. They, too, were hungry, and eggs usually figured large on their menu. Now, lying still on an outcrop of rock, they watched the rat sneaking along, occasionally sniffing at the air and finally vanishing behind a boulder. When he reappeared, he was struggling to roll an egg uphill towards his hole.

The rat was in difficulty, pushing the egg sometimes with his paws, sometimes with his nose. The ground was rough, and the egg wouldn't move straight. Deciding that he must have help, he scuttled off to call his spouse. Even now the mongooses did not descend on the tantalizing egg. They waited until the rat returned with his wife, and then watched as the male rat took the egg firmly between his forepaws and rolled over on to his back. The female rat then grabbed her mate's tail and began to drag him along.

Totally absorbed in the struggle with the egg, the rat did not hear the approach of the mongooses. When these two large furry visitors suddenly bobbed up from behind a stone, the rats squealed with fright, abandoned the egg, and fled for their lives.

The mongooses wasted no time in breaking open the egg and making a meal of it. But just as, a few minutes ago, the rat had not noticed their approach, so now they did not notice the village boy, carrying a small bright axe and a net bag in his hands, creeping along.

Ramu, too, was searching for eggs, and when he saw the mongooses busy with one, he stood still to watch them, his eyes roving in search of the nest. He was hoping the mongooses would lead him to the nest; but, when they had finished their meal and made off into the undergrowth, Ramu had to do his own searching. He failed to find the nest, and moved further into the forest. The rat's hopes were just reviving when, to his disgust, the mother hen returned.

Ramu now made his way to a mahua tree.

The flowers of the mahua can be eaten by animals as well as by men. Bears are particularly fond of them and will eat large quantities of flowers, which gradually start fermenting in their stomachs with the result that the animals get quite drunk. Ramu had often seen a couple of bears stumbling home to their cave, bumping into each other or into the trunks of trees. They are short-sighted to begin with, and when drunk can hardly see at all. But their sense of smell and hearing are so good that in the end they find their way home.

Ramu decided he would gather some mahua flowers, and

climbed up the tree, which is leafless when it blossoms. He began breaking the white flowers and throwing them to the ground. He had been on the tree for about five minutes when he heard the whining grumble of a bear, and presently a young sloth bear ambled into the clearing beneath the tree.

He was a small bear, little more than a cub, and Ramu was not frightened; but, because he thought the mother might be in the vicinity, he decided to take no chances, and sat very still, waiting to see what the bear would do. He hoped it wouldn't choose the mahua tree for a meal.

At first, the young bear put his nose to the ground and sniffed his way along until he came to a large anthill. Here he began huffing and puffing, blowing rapidly in and out of his nostrils, causing the dust from the anthill to fly in all directions. But he was a disappointed bear, because the anthill had been deserted long ago. And so, grumbling, he made his way across to a tall wild plum tree, and shinning rapidly up the smooth trunk, was soon perched on its topmost branches. It was only then that he saw Ramu.

The bear at once scrambled several feet higher up the tree, and laid himself out flat on a branch. It wasn't a very thick branch and left a large expanse of bear showing on either side. The bear tucked his head away behind another branch, and so long as he could not see Ramu, seemed quite satisfied that he was well hidden, though he couldn't help grumbling with anxiety, for a bear, like most animals, is afraid of man.

Bears, however, are also very curious—and curiosity has often led them into trouble. Slowly, inch by inch, the young bear's black snout appeared over the edge of the branch; but as soon as the eyes came into view and met Ramu's, he drew back with a jerk and the head was once more hidden. The bear did this two or three times, and Ramu, highly amused, waited until it wasn't looking, then moved some way down the tree. When the bear looked up again and saw that the boy was missing, he was so pleased with himself that he stretched right across to the next branch, to get a plum. Ramu chose this moment to burst into loud laughter. The startled bear tumbled out of the tree, dropped through the branches for a distance of some fifteen feet, and landed with a thud in a heap of dry leaves.

And then several things happened at almost the same time.

The mother bear came charging into the clearing. Spotting Ramu in the tree, she reared up on her hind legs, grunting fiercely. It was Ramu's turn to be startled. There are few animals more dangerous than a rampaging mother bear, and the boy knew that one blow from her clawed forepaws could rip his skull open.

But before the bear could approach the tree, there was a tremendous roar, and the old tiger bounded into the clearing. He had been asleep in the bushes not far away—he liked a good sleep after a heavy meal—and the noise in the clearing had woken him.

He was in a bad mood, and his loud *'A-oonh!'* made his displeasure quite clear. The bears turned and ran from the clearing, the youngster squealing with fright.

The tiger then came into the centre of the clearing, looked up at the trembling boy, and roared again.

Ramu nearly fell out of the tree.

'Good day to you, Uncle,' he stammered, showing his teeth in a nervous grin.

Perhaps this was too much for the tiger. With a low growl, he turned his back on the mahua tree and padded off into the jungle, his tail twitching in disgust.

That night, when Ramu told his parents and his grandfather about the tiger and how he had saved him from a female bear, it started a round of tiger stories—about how some of them could be gentlemen, others rogues. Sooner or later the conversation came round to man-eaters, and Grandfather told two stories which he swore were true, although his listeners only half believed him.

The first story concerned the belief that a man-eating tiger is guided towards his next victim by the spirit of a human being previously killed and eaten by the tiger. Grandfather said that he actually knew three hunters who sat up in a machan over a human kill, and when the tiger came, the corpse sat up and pointed with his right hand at the men in the tree. The tiger then went away. But the hunters knew he would return, and one man was brave enough to get down from the tree and tie the right arm of the corpse to its side. Later, when the tiger returned, the corpse sat up and this time pointed out the men with his left hand. The enraged tiger sprang into the tree and killed his enemies in the machan.

'And then there was a bania,' said Grandfather, beginning another story, 'who lived in a village in the jungle. He wanted to visit a neighbouring village to collect some money that was owed to him, but as the road lay through heavy forest in which lived a terrible man-eating tiger, he did not know what to do. Finally, he went to a sadhu, who gave him two powders. By eating the first powder he could turn into a huge tiger, capable of dealing with any other tiger in the jungle, and by eating the second he would become a bania again.

'Armed with his two powders, and accompanied by his pretty, young wife, the bania set out on his journey. They had not gone far into the forest when they came upon the man-eater sitting in the middle of the road. Before swallowing the first powder, the bania told his wife to stay where she was, so that when he returned after killing the tiger, she could at once give him the second powder and enable him to resume his old shape.

'Well, the bania's plan worked, but only up to a point. He swallowed the first powder and immediately became a magnificent tiger. With a great roar, he bounded towards the man-eater, and after a brief, furious fight, killed his opponent. Then, with his jaws still dripping blood, he returned to his wife.

'The poor girl was terrified and spilt the second powder on the ground. The bania was so angry that he pounced on his wife and killed and ate her. And afterwards, this terrible tiger was so enraged at not being able to become a human again that he killed and ate hundreds of people all over the country.'

'The only people he spared,' added Grandfather, with a twinkle in his eyes, 'were those who owed him money. A bania never gives up a loan as lost, and the tiger still hoped that one day he might become a human again and be able to collect his dues.'

Next morning, when Ramu came back from the well which was used to irrigate his father's fields, he found a crowd of curious children surrounding a jeep and three strangers with guns. Each of the strangers had a gun, and they were accompanied by two bearers and a vast amount of provisions.

They had heard that there was a tiger in the area, and they wanted to shoot it.

One of the hunters, who looked even more strange than the others, had come all the way from America to shoot a tiger, and he vowed that he would not leave the country without a tiger's skin in his baggage. One of his companions had said that he could buy a tiger's skin in Delhi, but the hunter said he preferred to get his own trophies.

These men had money to spend, and as most of the villagers needed money badly, they were only too willing to go into the forest to construct a machan for the hunters. The platform, big enough to take the three men, was put up in the branches of a tall toon, or mahogany, tree.

It was the only night the hunters used the machan. At the end of March, though the days are warm, the nights are still cold. The hunters had neglected to bring blankets, and by midnight, their teeth were chattering. Ramu, having tied up a buffalo calf for them at the foot of the tree, made as if to go home but instead circled the area, hanging up bits and pieces of old clothing on small trees and bushes. He thought he owed that much to the tiger. He knew the wily old king of the jungle would keep well away from the bait if he saw the bits of clothing—for where there were men's clothes, there would be men.

The vigil lasted well into the night but the tiger did not come near the toon tree. Perhaps he wasn't hungry; perhaps he got Ramu's message. In any case, the men in the tree soon gave themselves away.

The cold was really too much for them. A flask of rum was produced, and passed round, and it was not long before there was more purpose to finishing the rum than to finishing off a tiger. Silent at first, the men soon began talking in whispers; and to jungle creatures a human whisper is as telling as a trumpet call.

Soon the men were quite merry, talking in loud voices. And when the first morning light crept over the forest, and Ramu and his friends came back to fetch the great hunters, they found them fast asleep in the machan.

The hunters looked surly and embarrassed as they trudged back to the village.

'No game left in these parts,' said the American.

'Wrong time of the year for tiger,' said the second man.

'Don't know what the country's coming to,' said the third.

And complaining about the weather, the poor quality of

cartridges, the quantity of rum they had drunk, and the perversity of tigers, they drove away in disgust.

It was not until the onset of summer that an event occurred which altered the hunting habits of the old tiger and brought him into conflict with the villagers.

There had been no rain for almost two months, and the tall jungle grass had become a sea of billowy dry yellow. Some refugee settlers, living in an area where the forest had been cleared, had been careless while cooking and had started a jungle fire. Slowly it spread into the interior, from where the acrid smell and the fumes smoked the tiger out towards the edge of the jungle. As night came on, the flames grew more vivid, and the smell stronger. The tiger turned and made for the jheel, where he knew he would be safe provided he swam across to the little island in the centre.

Next morning he was on the island, which was untouched by the fire. But his surroundings had changed. The slopes of the hills were black with burnt grass, and most of the tall bamboo had disappeared. The deer and the wild pig, finding that their natural cover had gone, fled further east.

When the fire had died down and the smoke had cleared, the tiger prowled through the forest again but found no game. Once he came across the body of a burnt rabbit, but he could not eat it. He drank at the jheel and settled down in a shady spot to sleep the day away. Perhaps, by evening, some of the animals would return. If not, he, too, would have to look for new hunting grounds—or new game.

The tiger spent five more days looking for suitable game to kill. By that time he was so hungry that he even resorted to rooting among the dead leaves and burnt out stumps of trees, searching for worms and beetles. This was a sad comedown for the king of the jungle. But even now he hesitated to leave the area, for he had a deep suspicion and fear of the forest further east—forests that were fast being swallowed up by human habitation. He could have gone north, into high mountains, but they did not provide him with the long grass he needed. A panther could manage quite well up there, but not a tiger, who loved the natural privacy of the heavy jungle. In the hills, he would have to hide all the time.

At break of day, the tiger came to the jheel. The water was now shallow and muddy, and a green scum had spread over the top. But it was still drinkable and the tiger quenched his thirst.

He lay down across his favourite rock, hoping for a deer but none came. He was about to get up and go away when he heard an animal approach.

The tiger at once leaped off his perch and flattened himself on the ground, his tawny striped skin merging with the dry grass. A heavy animal was moving through the bushes, and the tiger waited patiently.

A buffalo emerged and came to the water.

The buffalo was alone.

He was a big male, and his long curved horns lay right back across his shoulders. He moved leisurely towards the water, completely unaware of the tiger's presence.

The tiger hesitated before making his charge. It was a long time—many years—since he had killed a buffalo, and he knew the villagers would not like it. But the pangs of hunger overcame his scruples. There was no morning breeze, everything was still, and the smell of the tiger did not reach the buffalo. A monkey chattered on a nearby tree, but his warning went unheeded.

Crawling stealthily on his stomach, the tiger skirted the edge of the jheel and approached the buffalo from the rear. The waterbirds, who were used to the presence of both animals, did not raise an alarm.

Getting closer, the tiger glanced around to see if there were men, or other buffaloes, in the vicinity. Then, satisfied that he was alone, he crept forward. The buffalo was drinking, standing in shallow water at the edge of the jheel, when the tiger charged from the side and bit deep into the animal's thigh.

The buffalo turned to fight, but the tendons of his right hind leg had been snapped, and he could only stagger forward a few paces. But he was a buffalo—the bravest of the domestic cattle. He was not afraid. He snorted, and lowered his horns at the tiger; but the great cat was too fast, and circling the buffalo, bit into the other hind leg.

The buffalo crashed to the ground, both hind legs crippled, and then the tiger dashed in, using both tooth and claw, biting deep into the buffalo's throat until the blood gushed out from the jugular vein.

The buffalo gave one long, last bellow before dying.

The tiger, having rested, now began to gorge himself, but, even though he had been starving for days, he could not finish the huge carcass. At least one good meal still remained when, satisfied and feeling his strength returning, he quenched his thirst at the jheel. Then he dragged the remains of the buffalo into the bushes to hide it from the vultures, and went off to find a place to sleep.

He would return to the kill when he was hungry.

The villagers were upset when they discovered that a buffalo was missing; and the next day, when Ramu and Shyam came running home to say that they had found the carcass near the jheel, half eaten by a tiger, the men were disturbed and angry. They felt that the tiger had tricked and deceived them. And they knew that once he got a taste for domestic cattle, he would make a habit of slaughtering them.

Kundan Singh, Shyam's father and the owner of the dead buffalo, said he would go after the tiger himself.

'It is all very well to talk about what you will do to the tiger,' said his wife, 'but you should never have let the buffalo go off on its own.'

'He had been out on his own before,' said Kundan. 'This is the first time the tiger has attacked one of our beasts. A devil must have entered the maharaja.'

'He must have been very hungry,' said Shyam.

'Well, we are hungry too,' said Kundan Singh.

'Our best buffalo—the only male in our herd.'

'The tiger will kill again,' said Ramu's father.

'If we let him,' said Kundan.

'Should we send for the shikaris?'

'No. They were not clever. The tiger will escape them easily. Besides, there is no time. The tiger will return for another meal tonight. We must finish him off ourselves!'

'But how?'

Kundan Singh smiled secretively, played with the ends of his moustache for a few moments, and then, with great pride, produced from under his cot a double-barrelled gun of ancient vintage.

'My father bought it from an Englishman,' he said.

'How long ago was that?'

'At the time I was born.'

'And have you ever used it?' asked Ramu's father, who was not sure that the gun would work.

'Well, some years back I let it off at some bandits. You remember the time when those dacoits raided our village? They chose the wrong village, and were severely beaten for their pains. As they left, I fired my gun off at them. They didn't stop running until they crossed the Ganga!'

'Yes, but did you hit anyone?'

'I would have, if someone's goat hadn't got in the way at the last moment. But we had roast mutton that night! Don't worry, brother, I know how the thing fires.'

Accompanied by Ramu's father and some others, Kundan Singh set out for the jheel, where, without shifting the buffalo's carcass—for they knew that the tiger would not come near them if he suspected a trap—they made another machan in the branches of a tall tree some thirty feet from the kill.

Later that evening, Kundan Singh and Ramu's father settled down for the night on their crude platform in the tree.

Several hours passed, and nothing but a jackal was seen by the watchers. And then, just as the moon came up over the distant hills, Kundan and his companion were startled by a low 'A-oonh!', followed by a suppressed, rumbling growl.

Kundan grasped his old gun, whilst his friend drew closer to him for comfort. There was complete silence for a minute or two—time that was an agony of suspense for the watchers—and then the sound of stealthy footfalls on dead leaves under the trees.

A moment later, the tiger walked out into the moonlight and stood over his kill.

At first Kundan could do nothing. He was completely overawed by the size of this magnificent tiger. Ramu's father had to nudge him, and then Kundan quickly put the gun to his shoulder, aimed at the tiger's head, and pressed the trigger.

The gun went off with a flash and two loud bangs, as Kundan fired both barrels. Then there was a tremendous roar. One of the bullets had grazed the tiger's head.

The enraged animal rushed at the tree and tried to leap up into the branches. Fortunately, the machan had been built at a safe height, and the tiger was unable to reach it. He roared again and then bounded off into the forest.

'What a tiger!' exclaimed Kundan, half in fear and half in admiration. 'I feel as though my liver has turned to water.'

'You missed him completely,' said Ramu's father. 'Your gun makes a big noise; an arrow would have done more damage.'

'I did not miss him,' said Kundan, feeling offended. 'You heard him roar, didn't you? Would he have been so angry if he had not been hit? If I have wounded him badly, he will die.'

'And if you have wounded him slightly, he may turn into a man-eater, and then where will we be?'

'I don't think he will come back,' said Kundan. 'He will leave these forests.'

They waited until the sun was up before coming down from the tree. They found a few drops of blood on the dry grass but no trail led into the forest, and Ramu's father was convinced that the wound was only a slight one.

The bullet, missing the fatal spot behind the ear, had only grazed the back of the skull and cut a deep groove at its base. It took a few days to heal, and during this time the tiger lay low and did not go near the jheel except when it was very dark and he was very thirsty.

The villagers thought the tiger had gone away, and Ramu and Shyam—accompanied by some other youths, and always carrying axes and lathis—began bringing buffaloes to the jheel again during the day; but they were careful not to let any of them stray far from the herd, and they returned home while it was still daylight.

It was some days since the jungle had been ravaged by the fire, and in the tropics the damage is repaired quickly. In spite of it being the dry season, new life was creeping into the forest.

While the buffaloes wallowed in the muddy water, and the boys wrestled on the grassy island, a big tawny eagle soared high above them, looking for a meal—a sure sign that some of the animals were beginning to return to the forest. It was not long before his keen eyes detected a movement in the glade below.

What the eagle with his powerful eyesight saw was a baby hare, a small fluffy thing, its long pink-tinted ears laid flat along its sides. Had it not been creeping along between two large stones, it would have escaped notice. The eagle waited to see if the mother was about, and as he waited he realized that he was not the only one who coveted this juicy morsel. From the bushes there had appeared a sinuous yellow creature, pressed, low to the ground and moving rapidly towards the hare. It was a yellow jungle cat, hardly noticeable in the scorched grass. With great stealth the jungle cat began to stalk the baby hare.

He pounced. The hare's squeal was cut short by the cat's cruel claws; but it had been heard by the mother hare, who now bounded into the glade and without the slightest hesitation went for the surprised cat.

There was nothing haphazard about the mother hare's attack. She flashed around behind the cat and jumped clean over him. As she landed, she kicked back, sending a stinging jet of dust shooting into the cat's face. She did this again and again.

The bewildered cat, crouching and snarling, picked up the kill and tried to run away with it. But the hare would not permit this. She continued her leaping and buffeting, till eventually the cat, out of sheer frustration, dropped the kill and attacked the mother.

The cat sprang at the hare a score of times, lashing out with his claws; but the mother hare was both clever and agile enough to keep just out of reach of those terrible claws, and drew the cat further and further away from her baby—for she did not as yet know that it was dead.

The tawny eagle saw his chance. Swift and true, he swooped. For a brief moment, as his wings overspread the furry small little hare and his talons sank deep into it, he caught a glimpse of the cat racing towards him and the mother hare fleeing into the bushes. And then with a shrill '*kee-ee-ee*' of triumph, he rose and whirled away with his dinner.

The boys had heard his shrill cry and looked up just in time to see the eagle flying over the jheel with the little hare held firmly in his talons.

'Poor hare,' said Shyam. 'Its life was short.'

'That's the law of the jungle,' said Ramu. 'The eagle has a family, too, and must feed it.'

'I wonder if we are any better than animals,' said Shyam.

'Perhaps we are a little better, in some ways,' said Ramu. 'Grandfather always says, "To be able to laugh and to be merciful are the only things that make man better than the beast."'

The next day, while the boys were taking the herd home, one of the buffaloes lagged behind. Ramu did not realize that the animal was missing until he heard an agonized bellow behind him. He glanced over his shoulder just in time to see the big striped tiger dragging the buffalo into a clump of young bamboo. At the same time, the herd became aware of the danger, and the buffaloes snorted with fear as they hurried along the forest path. To urge them forward, and to warn his friends, Ramu cupped his hands to his mouth and gave vent to a yodelling call.

The buffaloes bellowed, the boys shouted, and the birds flew shrieking from the trees. It was almost a stampede by the time the herd emerged from the forest. The villagers heard the thunder of hoofs, and saw the herd coming home amidst clouds of dust and confusion, and knew that something was wrong.

'The tiger!' shouted Ramu. 'He is here! He has killed one of the buffaloes.'

'He is afraid of us no longer,' said Shyam.

'Did you see where he went?' asked Kundan Singh, hurrying up to them.

'I remember the place,' said Ramu. 'He dragged the buffalo in amongst the bamboo.'

'Then there is no time to lose,' said his father. 'Kundan, you take your gun and two men, and wait near the suspension bridge, where the Garur stream joins the Ganga. The jungle is narrow there. We will beat the jungle from our side, and drive the tiger towards you. He will not escape us, unless he swims the river!'

'Good!' said Kundan Singh, running into his house for his gun, with Shyam close at his heels. 'Was it one of our buffaloes again?' he asked.

'It was Ramu's buffalo this time,' said Shyam. 'A good milk buffalo.'

'Then Ramu's father will beat the jungle thoroughly. You boys had better come with me. It will not be safe for you to accompany the beaters.'

Kundan Singh, carrying his gun and accompanied by Ramu, Shyam and two men, headed for the river junction, while Ramu's father collected about twenty men from the village and, guided by one of the boys who had been with Ramu, made for the spot where the tiger had killed the buffalo.

The tiger was still eating when he heard the men coming. He had not expected to be disturbed so soon. With an angry 'Whoof!' he bounded into a bamboo thicket and watched the men through a screen of leaves and tall grass.

The men did not seem to take much notice of the dead buffalo, but gathered round their leader and held a consultation. Most of them carried hand drums slung from their shoulders. They also carried sticks, spears and axes.

After a hurried conversation, they entered the denser part of the jungle, beating their drums with the palms of their hands. Some of the men banged empty kerosene tins. These made even more noise than the drums.

The tiger did not like the noise and retreated deeper into the jungle. But he was surprised to find that the men, instead of going away, came after him into the jungle, banging away on their drums and tins, and shouting at the top of their voices. They had separated now, and advanced single or in pairs, but nowhere were they more than fifteen yards apart. The tiger could easily have broken through this slowly advancing semicircle of men—one swift blow from his paw would have felled the strongest of them—but his main aim was to get away from the noise. He hated and feared noise made by men.

He was not a man-eater and he would not attack a man unless he was very angry or frightened or very desperate; and he was none of these things as yet. He had eaten well, and he would have liked to rest in peace—but there would be no rest for any animal until the men ceased their tremendous clatter and din.

For an hour Ramu's father and the others beat the jungle, calling, drumming and trampling the undergrowth. The tiger had no rest. Whenever he was able to put some distance between himself and the men, he would sink down in some shady spot to rest; but, within five or ten minutes, the trampling and drumming would sound nearer, and the tiger, with an angry snarl, would get up and pad north, pad silently north along the narrowing strip of jungle, towards the junction of the Garur stream and the Ganga. Ten years ago, he would have had the jungle on his right in which to hide; but the trees had been felled long ago to make way for humans and houses, and now he could only move to the left, towards the river.

It was about noon when the tiger finally appeared in the open. He longed for the darkness and security of the night, for the sun was his enemy. Kundan and the boys had a clear view of him as he stalked slowly along—now in the open with the sun glinting on his glossy hide, now in the shade or passing through the shorter reeds. He was still out of range of Kundan's gun, but there was no fear of his getting out of the beat, as the 'stops' were all picked men from the village. He disappeared among some bushes but soon reappeared to retrace his steps, the beaters having done their work well. He was now only one hundred and fifty yards from the rocks where Kundan Singh waited, and he looked very big.

The beat had closed in, and the exit along the bank downstream was completely blocked, so the tiger turned and disappeared into a belt of reeds, and Kundan Singh expected that the head would soon peer out of the cover a few yards away. The beaters were now making a great noise, shouting and beating their drums, but nothing moved; and Ramu, watching from a distance, wondered, 'Has he slipped through the beaters?' And he half hoped so.

Tins clashed, drums beat, and some of the men poked into the reeds with their spears or long bamboos. Perhaps one of these thrusts found a mark, because at last the tiger was roused, and with an angry desperate snarl, he charged out of the reeds, splashing his way through an inlet of mud and water. Kundan Singh fired, and his bullet struck the tiger on the thigh.

The mighty animal stumbled; but he was up in a minute, and rushing through a gap in the narrowing line of beaters, he made straight for the only way across the river—the suspension bridge that passed over the Ganga here, providing a route into the high hills beyond.

'We'll get him now,' said Kundan, priming his gun again. 'He's right in the open!'

The suspension bridge swayed and trembled as the wounded

tiger lurched across it. Kundan fired, and this time the bullet grazed the tiger's shoulder. The animal bounded forward, lost his footing on the unfamiliar, slippery planks of the swaying bridge, and went over the side, falling headlong into the strong, swirling waters of the river.

He rose to the surface once, but the current took him under and away, and only a thin streak of blood remained on the river's surface.

Kundan and others hurried downstream to see if the dead tiger had been washed up on the river's banks; but though they searched the riverside for several miles, they did not find the king of the forest.

He had not provided anyone with a trophy. His skin would not be spread on a couch, nor would his head be hung up on a wall. No claw of his would be hung as a charm round the neck of a child. No villager would use his fat as a cure for rheumatism.

At first the villagers were glad because they felt their buffaloes were safe. Then the men began to feel that something had gone out of their lives, out of the life of the forest; they began to feel that the forest was no longer a forest. It had been shrinking year by year, but, as long as the tiger had been there and the villagers had heard it roar at night, they had known that they were still secure from the intruders and newcomers who came to fell the trees and eat up the land and let the flood waters into the village. But now that the tiger had gone, it was as though a protector had gone, leaving the forest open and vulnerable, easily destroyable. And once the forest was destroyed they, too, would be in danger…

There was another thing that had gone with the tiger, another thing that had been lost, a thing that was being lost everywhere—something called 'nobility'.

Ramu remembered something that his grandfather had once said. 'The tiger is the very soul of India, and when the last tiger goes, so will the soul of the country.'

The boys lay flat on their stomachs on their little mud island and watched the monsoon clouds gathering overhead.

'The king of our forest is dead,' said Shyam. 'There are no more tigers.'

'There must be tigers,' said Ramu. 'How can there be an India without tigers?'

The river had carried the tiger many miles away from his home, from the forest he had always known, and brought him ashore on a strip of warm yellow sand, where he lay in the sun, quite still, but breathing.

Vultures gathered and waited at a distance, some of them perching on the branches of nearby trees.

But the tiger was more drowned than hurt, and as the river water oozed out of his mouth, and the warm sun made new life throb through his body, he stirred and stretched, and his glazed eyes came into focus. Raising his head, he saw trees and tall grass.

Slowly, he heaved himself off the ground and moved at a crouch to where the grass waved in the afternoon breeze. Would he be harried again, and shot at? There was no smell of man. The tiger moved forward with greater confidence.

There was, however, another smell in the air—a smell that reached back to the time when he was young and fresh and full of vigour—a smell that he had almost forgotten but could never quite forget: the smell of a tigress!

He raised his head high, and new life surged through his tired limbs. He gave a full-throated roar and moved purposefully through the tall grass. And the roar came back to him, calling him, calling him forward: a roar that meant there would be more tigers in the land!

Exciting Encounters

A Crow for All Seasons

Early to bed and early to rise makes a crow healthy, wealthy, and wise.

They say it's true for humans too. I'm not so sure about that. But for crows it's a must.

I'm always up at the crack of dawn, often the first crow to break the night's silence with a lusty caw. My friends and relatives, who roost in the same tree, grumble a bit and mutter to themselves, but they are soon cawing just as loudly. Long before the sun is up, we set off on the day's work.

We do not pause even for the morning wash. Later in the day, if it's hot and muggy, I might take a dip in some human's bath water; but early in the morning we like to be up and about before everyone else. This is the time when trash cans and refuse dumps are overflowing with goodies, and we like to sift through them before the dustmen arrive in their disposal trucks.

Not that we are afraid of a famine in refuse. As human beings multiply, so does their rubbish.

Only yesterday I rescued an old typewriter ribbon from the dustbin, just before it was emptied. What a waste that would have been! I had no use for it myself, but I gave it to one of my cousins who got married recently, and she tells me it's just right for her nest, the one she's building on a telegraph pole. It helps her bind the twigs together, she says.

My own preference is for toothbrushes. They're just a hobby really, like stamp-collecting with humans. I have a small but select collection which I keep in a hole in the garden wall. Don't ask me how many I've got—crows don't believe there's any point in counting beyond two—but I know there's more than *one,* that there's a whole lot of them in fact, because there isn't anyone living on this road who hasn't lost a toothbrush to me at some time or another.

We crows living in the jackfruit tree have this stretch of road to ourselves, but so that we don't quarrel or have misunderstandings we've shared the houses out. I picked the bungalow with the orchard at the back. After all, I don't eat rubbish and throwaways all the time. Just occasionally, I like a ripe guava or the soft flesh of a papaya. And sometimes I like the odd beetle as an hors d'oeuvre. Those humans in the bungalow should be grateful to me for keeping down the population of fruit-eating beetles, and even for recycling their refuse; but no, humans are never grateful. No sooner do I settle in one of their guava trees than stones are whizzing past me. So I return to the dustbin on the back veranda steps. They don't mind my being there.

One of my cousins shares the bungalow with me, but he's a lazy fellow and I have to do most of the foraging. Sometimes I get him to lend me a claw, but most of the time he's preening his feathers and trying to look handsome for a pretty young thing who lives in the banyan tree at the next turning.

When he's in the mood he can be invaluable, as he proved recently when I was having some difficulty getting at the dog's food on the veranda.

This dog, who is fussed over so much by the humans, I've adopted is a great big fellow, a mastiff who pretends to a pedigree going back to the time of Genghis Khan—he likes to pretend one of his ancestors was the great Khan's watchdog. But, as often happens in famous families, animal or human, there is a falling off in quality over a period of time, and this huge fellow—Tiger, they call him—is a case in point. All brawn and no brain. Many's the time I've removed a juicy bone from his plate or helped myself to pickings from under his nose.

But of late he's been growing canny and selfish. He doesn't like to share any more. And the other day I was almost in his jaws when he took a sudden lunge at me. Snap went his great teeth; but all he got was one of my tail feathers. He spat it out in disgust. Who wants crow's meat, anyway?

All the same, I thought, I'd better not be too careless. It's not for nothing that a crow's IQ is way above that of all other birds. And it's higher than a dog's, I bet.

I woke Cousin Slow from his midday siesta and said, 'Hey, Slow, we've got a problem. If you want any of that delicious tripe today, you've got to lend a claw—or a beak. That dog's getting snappier day by day.'

Slow opened one eye and said, 'Well, if you insist. But you know how I hate getting into a scuffle. It's bad for the gloss on my feathers.'

'I don't insist,' I said politely. 'But I'm not foraging for both of us today. It's every crow for himself.'

'Okay, okay, I'm coming,' said Slow, and with barely a flap he dropped down from the tree to the wall.

'What's the strategy?' I asked.

'Simple. We'll just give him the old one-two.'

We flew across to the veranda. Tiger had just started his meal. He was a fast, greedy eater who made horrible slurping sounds while he guzzled his food. We had to move fast if we wanted to get something before the meal was over.

I sidled up to Tiger and wished him good afternoon.

He kept on gobbling—but quicker now.

Slow came up from behind and gave him a quick peck near the tail—a sensitive spot—and, as Tiger swung round, snarling, I moved in quickly and snatched up several tidbits.

Tiger went for me, and I flew freestyle for the garden wall. The dish was untended, so Slow helped himself to as many scraps as he could stuff in his mouth.

He joined me on the garden wall, and we sat there feasting, while Tiger barked himself hoarse below.

'Go catch a cat,' said Slow, who is given to slang. 'You're in the wrong league, big boy.'

The great sage Pratyasataka—ever heard of him? I guess not—once said, 'Nothing can improve a crow.'

Like most human sages he wasn't very clear in his thinking, so that there has been some misunderstanding about what he meant. Humans like to think that what he really meant was that crows were so bad as to be beyond improvement. But we crows know better. We interpret the saying as meaning that the crow is so perfect that no improvement is possible.

It's not that we aren't human—what I mean is, there are times when we fall from our high standards and do rather foolish things. Like at lunchtime the other day.

Sometimes, when the table is laid in the bungalow, and before the family enters the dining room, I nip in through the open window and make a quick foray among the dishes. Sometimes I'm lucky enough to pick up a sausage or a slice of toast, or even a pat of butter, making off before someone enters and throws a bread knife at me. But on this occasion, just as I was reaching for the toast, a thin slouching fellow—Junior Sahib they call him—entered suddenly and shouted at me. I was so startled that I leapt across the table seeking shelter. Something flew at me, and in an effort to dodge the missile, I put my head through a circular object and then found it wouldn't come off.

It wasn't safe to hang around there, so I flew out the window with this dashed ring still round my neck.

Serviette or napkin rings, that's what they are called. Quite unnecessary objects, but some humans—particularly the well-to-do sort—seem to like having them on their tables, holding bits of cloth in place. The cloth is used for wiping the mouth. Have you ever heard of such nonsense?

Anyway, there I was with a fat napkin ring round my neck, and as I perched on the wall trying to get it off, the entire human family gathered on their veranda to watch me.

There was the Colonel Sahib and his wife, the Memsahib; there was the scrawny Junior Sahib (worst of the lot); there was a mischievous boy (the Colonel Sahib's grandson) known as the Baba; there was the cook (who usually flung orange peels at me) and the gardener (who once tried to decapitate me with a spade), and the dog Tiger who, like most dogs, tries unsuccessfully to be human.

Today they weren't cursing and shaking their fists at me; they were just standing and laughing their heads off. What's so funny about a crow with its head stuck in a napkin ring?

Worse was to follow.

The noise had attracted the other crows in the area, and if there's one thing crows detest, it's a crow who doesn't look like a crow.

They swooped low and dived on me, hammering at the wretched napkin ring, until they had knocked me off the wall and into a flower bed. Then six or seven toughs landed on me with every intention of finishing me off.

'Hey, boys!' I cawed. 'This is me, Speedy! What are you trying to do—kill me?'

'That's right! You don't look like Speedy to us. What have you done with him, eh?'

And they set upon me with even greater vigour.

'You're just like a bunch of lousy humans!' I shouted. 'You're no better than them—this is just the way they carry on amongst themselves!'

That brought them to a halt. They stopped trying to peck me to pieces, and stood back, looking puzzled. The napkin ring had been shattered in the onslaught and had fallen to the ground.

'Why, it's Speedy!' said one of the gang.

'None other!'

'Good old Speedy—what are you doing here? And where's the guy we were hammering just now?'

There was no point in trying to explain things to them. Crows are like that. They're all good pals—until one of them tries to look different. Then he could be just another bird.

'He took off for Tibet,' I said. 'It was getting unhealthy for him around here.'

Summertime is here again. And although I'm a crow for all seasons, I must admit to a preference for the summer months.

Humans grow lazy and don't pursue me with so much vigour. Garbage cans overflow. Food goes bad and is constantly being thrown away. Overripe fruit gets tastier by the minute. If fellows like me weren't around to mop up all these unappreciated riches, how would humans manage?

There's one character in the bungalow, Junior Sahib, who will never appreciate our services, it seems. He simply hates crows. The small boy may throw stones at us occasionally, but then, he's the sort who throws stones at almost anything. There's nothing personal about it. He just throws stones on principle.

The Memsahib is probably the best of the lot. She often throws me scraps from the kitchen—onion skins, potato peels, crusts, and leftovers—and even when I nip in and make off with something not meant for me (like a jam tart or a cheese pakora) she is quite sporting about it. The Junior Sahib looks outraged, but the lady of the house says, 'Well, we've all got to make a living somehow, and that's how crows make theirs. It's high time you thought of earning a living.' Junior Sahib's her nephew—that's his occupation. He has never been known to work.

The Colonel Sahib has a sense of humour but it's often directed at me. He thinks I'm a comedian.

He discovered I'd been making off with the occasional egg from the egg basket on the veranda, and one day, without my knowledge, he made a substitution.

Right on top of the pile I found a smooth round egg, and before anyone could shout, 'Crow!' I'd made off with it. It was abnormally light. I put it down on the lawn and set about cracking it with my strong beak, but it would keep slipping away or bounding off into the bushes. Finally, I got it between my feet and gave it a good hard whack. It burst open, and to my utter astonishment, there was nothing inside!

I looked up and saw the old man standing on the veranda, doubled up with laughter.

'What are you laughing at?' asked the Memsahib, coming out to see what it was all about.

'It's that ridiculous crow!' guffawed the Colonel, pointing at me. 'You know he's been stealing our eggs. Well, I placed a ping pong ball on top of the pile, and he fell for it! He's been struggling with that ball for twenty minutes! That will teach him a lesson.'

It did. But I had my revenge later, when I pinched a brand new toothbrush from the Colonel's bathroom.

The Junior Sahib has no sense of humour at all. He idles about the house and grounds all day, whistling or singing to himself.

'Even that crow sings better than Uncle,' said the boy.

A truthful boy; but all he got for his honesty was a whack on the head from his uncle.

Anyway, as a gesture of appreciation, I perched on the garden wall and gave the family a rendering of my favourite crow song, which is my own composition. Here it is, translated for your benefit:

> *Oh, for the life of a crow!*
> *A bird who's in the know.*
> *Although we are cursed,*
> *We are never dispersed—*
> *We're always on the go!*
> *I know I'm a bit of a rogue*
> *(And my voice wouldn't pass for a brogue),*
> *But there's no one as sleek*
> *Or as neat with his beak—*
> *So they're putting my picture in* Vogue!
> *Oh, for the life of a crow!*
> *I reap what I never sow,*
> *They call me a thief,*
> *Pray I'll soon come to grief—*
> *But there's no getting rid of a crow!*

I gave it everything I had, and the humans—all of them on the lawn to enjoy the evening breeze, listened to me in silence, struck with wonder at my performance. When I had finished, I bowed and preened myself, waiting for the applause.

They stared at each other for a few seconds. Then the Junior Sahib stooped, picked up a bottle opener, and flung it at me.

Well, I ask you!

What can one say about humans? I do my best to defend them from all kinds of criticism, and this is what I get for my pains.

Anyway, I picked up the bottle opener and added it to my collection of odds and ends.

It was getting dark, and soon everyone was stumbling around, looking for another bottle opener. Junior Sahib's popularity was even lower than mine.

One day, Junior Sahib came home carrying a heavy shotgun. He pointed it at me a few times and I dived for cover. But he didn't fire. Probably I was out of range.

'He's only threatening you,' said Slow from the safety of the jamun tree, where he sat in the shadows. 'He probably doesn't know how to fire the thing.'

But I wasn't taking any chances. I'd seen a sly look on Junior Sahib's face, and I decided that he was trying to make me careless. So I stayed well out of range.

Then one evening, I received a visit from my cousin, Charm. He'd come to me for a loan. He wanted some new bottle tops for his collection and had brought me a mouldy old toothbrush to offer in exchange.

Charm landed on the garden wall, toothbrush in his break, and was waiting for me to join him there, when there was a flash and a tremendous bang. Charm was sent several feet into the air, and landed limp and dead in a flower bed.

'I've got him, I've got him!' shouted Junior Sahib. 'I've shot that blasted crow!'

Throwing away the gun, Junior Sahib ran out into the garden, overcome with joy. He picked up my fallen relative, and began running around the bungalow with his trophy.

The rest of the family had collected on the veranda.

'Drop that thing at once!' called the Memsahib.

'Uncle is doing a war dance,' observed the boy.

'It's unlucky to shoot a crow,' said the Colonel.

I thought it was time to take a hand in the proceedings and let everyone know that the *right* crow—the one and only Speedy—was alive and kicking. So I swooped down the jackfruit tree, dived through Junior Sahib's window, and emerged with one of his socks.

Triumphantly flaunting his dead crow, Junior Sahib came dancing up the garden path, then stopped dead when he saw me perched on the window sill, a sock in my beak. His jaw fell, his eyes bulged; he looked like the owl in the banyan tree.

'You shot the wrong crow!' shouted the Colonel, and everyone roared with laughter.

Before Junior Sahib could recover from the shock, I took off in a leisurely fashion and joined Slow on the wall.

Junior Sahib came rushing out with the gun, but by now it was too dark to see anything, and I heard the Memsahib telling the Colonel, 'You'd better take that gun away before he does himself a mischief.' So the Colonel took Junior Sahib indoors and gave him a brandy.

I composed a new song for Junior Sahib's benefit, and sang it to him outside his window early next morning:

> *I understand you want a crow*
> *To poison, shoot or smother;*
> *My fond salaams, but by your leave*
> *I'll substitute another;*
> *Allow me then, to introduce*
> *My most respected brother.*

Although I was quite understanding about the whole tragic mix-up—I was, after all, the family's very own house crow—my fellow crows were outraged at what had happened to Charm, and swore vengeance on Junior Sahib.

'*Corvus splendens!*' they shouted with great spirit, forgetting that this title had been bestowed on us by a human. In times of war, we forget how much we owe to our enemies.

Junior Sahib had only to step into the garden, and several crows would swoop down on him, screeching and swearing and aiming lusty blows at his head and hands. He took to coming out wearing a sola topi, and even then they knocked it off and drove him indoors. Once he tried lighting a cigarette on the veranda steps, when Slow swooped low across the porch and snatched it from his lips.

Junior Sahib shut himself up in his room, and smoked countless cigarettes—a sure sign that his nerves were going to pieces.

Every now and then, the Memsahib would come out and shoo us off; and because she wasn't an enemy, we obliged by retreating to the garden wall. After all, Slow and I depended on her for much of our board if not for our lodging. But Junior Sahib had only to show his face outside the house, and all the crows in the area would be after him like avenging furies.

'It doesn't look as though they are going to forgive you,' said the Memsahib.

'Elephants never forget, and crows never forgive,' said the Colonel.

'Would you like to borrow my catapult, Uncle?' asked the boy. 'Just for self-protection, you know.'

'Shut up,' said Junior Sahib and went to bed.

One day, he sneaked out of the back door and dashed across to the garage. A little later the family's old car, seldom used, came out of the garage with Junior Sahib at the wheel. He'd decided that if he couldn't take a walk in safety he'd go for a drive. All the windows were up.

No sooner had the car turned into the driveway than about a dozen crows dived down on it, crowding the bonnet and flapping in front of the windscreen. Junior Sahib couldn't see a thing. He swung the steering wheel left, right and centre, and the car went off the driveway, ripped through a hedge, crushed a bed of sweetpeas and came to a stop against the trunk of a mango tree.

Junior Sahib just sat there, afraid to open the door. The family had to come out of the house and rescue him.

'Are you all right?' asked the Colonel.

'I've bruised my knees,' said Junior Sahib.

'Never mind your knees,' said the Memsahib, gazing around at the ruin of her garden. 'What about my sweetpeas?'

'I think your uncle is going to have a nervous breakdown,' I heard the Colonel saying to the boy.

'What's that?' asked the boy. 'Is it the same as a car having a breakdown?'

'Well, not exactly… But you could call it a mind breaking down.'

Junior Sahib had been refusing to leave his room or take his meals. The family was worried about him. I was worried, too. Believe it or not, we crows are among the very few birds who sincerely desire the preservation of the human species.

'He needs a change,' said the Memsahib.

'A rest cure,' said the Colonel sarcastically. 'A rest from doing nothing.'

'Send him to Switzerland,' suggested the boy.

'We can't afford that. But we can take him up to a hill station.'

The nearest hill station was some fifty miles as the human drives (only ten as the crow flies). Many people went up there during the summer months. It wasn't fancied much by crows. For one thing, it was a tidy sort of place, and people lived in houses that were set fairly far apart. Opportunities for scavenging were limited. Also it was rather cold and the trees were inconvenient and uncomfortable. A friend of mine, who had spent a night in a pine tree, said he hadn't been able to sleep because of the prickly pine needles and the wind howling through the branches.

'Let's all go up for a holiday,' said the Memsahib. 'We can spend a week in a boarding house. All of us need a change.'

A few days later the house was locked up, and the family piled into the old car and drove off to the hills.

I had the grounds to myself.

The dog had gone too, and the gardener spent all day dozing in his hammock. There was no one around to trouble me.

'We've got the whole place to ourselves,' I told Slow.

'Yes, but what good is that? With everyone gone, there are no throwaways, giveaways and takeaways!'

'We'll have to try the house next door.'

'And be driven off by the other crows? That's not our territory, you know. We can go across to help them, or to ask for their help, but we're not supposed to take their pickings. It just isn't cricket, old boy.'

We could have tried the bazaar or the railway station, where there is always a lot of rubbish to be found, but there is also a lot of competition in those places. The station crows are gangsters. The bazaar crows are bullies. Slow and I had grown soft. We'd have been no match for the bad boys.

'I've just realized how much we depend on humans,' I said.

'We could go back to living in the jungle,' said Slow.

'No, that would be too much like hard work. We'd be

living on wild fruit most of the time. Besides, the jungle crows won't have anything to do with us now. Ever since we took up with humans, we became the outcasts of the bird world.'

'That means we're almost human.'

'You might say we have all their vices and none of their virtues.'

'Just a different set of values, old boy.'

'Like eating hens' eggs instead of crows' eggs. That's something in their favour. And while you're hanging around here waiting for the mangoes to fall, I'm off to locate our humans.'

Slow's beak fell open. He looked like—well, a hungry crow.

'Don't tell me you're going to follow them up to the hill station? You don't even know where they are staying.'

'I'll soon find out,' I said, and took off for the hills.

You'd be surprised at how simple it is to be a good detective, if only you put your mind to it. Of course, if Ellery Queen had been able to fly, he wouldn't have required fifteen chapters and his father's assistance to crack a case.

Swooping low over the hill station, it wasn't long before I spotted my humans' old car. It was parked outside a boarding house called Climber's Rest. I hadn't seen anyone climbing, but dozing in an armchair in the garden was my favourite human.

I perched on top of a colourful umbrella and waited for Junior Sahib to wake up. I decided it would be rather inconsiderate of me to disturb his sleep, so I waited patiently on the brolly, looking at him with one eye and keeping one eye on the house. He stirred uneasily, as though he'd suddenly had a bad dream; then he opened his eyes. I must have been the first thing he saw.

'Good morning,' I cawed in a friendly tone—always ready to forgive and forget, that's Speedy!

He leapt out of the armchair and ran into the house,

hollering at the top of his voice.

I supposed he hadn't been able to contain his delight at seeing me again. Humans can be funny that way. They'll hate you one day and love you the next.

Well, Junior Sahib ran all over the boarding house screaming: 'It's that crow, it's that crow! He's following me everywhere!'

Various people, including the family, ran outside to see what the commotion was about, and I thought it would be better to make myself scarce. So I flew to the top of a spruce tree and stayed very still and quiet.

'Crow! What crow?' said the Colonel.

'Our crow!' cried Junior Sahib. 'The one that persecutes me. I was dreaming of it just now, and when I opened my eyes, there it was, on the garden umbrella!'

'There's nothing there now,' said the Memsahib. 'You probably hadn't woken up completely.'

'He is having illusions again,' said the boy.

'Delusions,' corrected the Colonel.

'Now look here,' said the Memsahib, 'you'll have to pull yourself together. You'll take leave of your senses if you don't.'

'I tell you, it's here!' sobbed Junior Sahib. 'It's following me everywhere.'

'It's grown fond of Uncle,' said the boy. 'And it seems Uncle can't live without crows.'

Junior Sahib looked up with a wild glint in his eye.

'That's it!' he cried. 'I can't live without them. That's the answer to my problem. I don't hate crows—I love them!'

Everyone just stood around goggling at Junior Sahib.

'I'm feeling fine now,' he carried on. 'What a difference it makes if you can just do the opposite of what you've been doing before! I thought I hated crows. But all the time I really loved them!' And flapping his arms, and trying to caw like a crow, he went prancing about the garden.

'Now he thinks he's a crow,' said the boy. 'Is he still having delusions?'

'That's right,' said the Memsahib. 'Delusions of grandeur.'

After that, the family decided that there was no point in staying on in the hill station any longer. Junior Sahib had completed his rest cure. And even if he was the only one who believed himself cured, that was all right, because after all he was the one who mattered... If you're feeling fine, can there be anything wrong with you?

No sooner was everyone back in the bungalow than Junior Sahib took to hopping barefoot on the grass early every morning, all the time scattering food about for the crows. Bread, chapattis, cooked rice, curried eggplants, the Memsahib's homemade toffee—you name it, we got it!

Slow and I were the first to help ourselves to these dawn offerings, and soon the other crows had joined us on the lawn. We didn't mind. Junior Sahib brought enough for everyone.

'We ought to honour him in some way,' said Slow.

'Yes, why not?' said I. 'There was someone else, hundreds of years ago, who fed the birds. They followed him wherever he went.'

'That's right. They made him a saint. But as far as I know, he didn't feed any crows. At least, you don't see any crows in the pictures—just sparrows and robins and wagtails.'

'Small fry. *Our* human is dedicated exclusively to crows. Do you realize that, Slow?'

'Sure. We ought to make him the patron saint of crows. What do you say, fellows?'

'*Caw, caw, caw!*' All the crows were in agreement.

'St Corvus!' said Slow as Junior Sahib emerged from the house, laden with good things to eat.

'*Corvus, corvus, corvus!*' we cried.

And what a pretty picture he made—a crow eating from his hand, another perched on his shoulder, and about a dozen of us on the grass, forming a respectful ring around him.

From persecutor to protector; from beastliness to saintliness. And sometimes it can be the other way round: you never know with humans!

Harold: Our Hornbill

HAROLD'S MOTHER, like all good hornbills, was the most careful of wives. His father was the most easy-going of husbands. In January, long before the flame tree flowered, Harold's father took his wife into a great hole high in the tree trunk, where his father and his father's father had taken their brides at the same time every year.

In this weather-beaten hollow, generation upon generation of hornbills had been raised. Harold's mother, like those before her, was enclosed within the hole by a sturdy wall of earth, sticks and dung.

Harold's father left a small hole in the centre of this wall to enable him to communicate with his wife whenever he felt like a chat. Walled up in her uncomfortable room, Harold's mother was a prisoner for over two months. During this period an egg was laid, and Harold was born.

In his naked boyhood Harold was no beauty. His most promising feature was his flaming red bill, matching the blossoms of the flame tree which was now ablaze, heralding the summer. He had a stomach that could never be filled, despite the best efforts of his parents who brought him pieces of jackfruit and berries from the banyan tree.

As he grew bigger, the room became more cramped, and one day his mother burst through the wall, spread out her wings and sailed over the tree-tops. Her husband was glad to see her about. He played with her, expressing his delight with deep gurgles and throaty chuckles. Then they repaired the wall of the nursery, so that Harold would not fall out.

Harold was quite happy in his cell, and felt no urge for freedom. He was putting on weight and a philosophy of his own. Then something happened to change the course of his life.

One afternoon he was awakened from his siesta by a loud thumping on the wall, a sound quite different from that made by his parents. Soon the wall gave way, and there was something large and yellow and furry staring at him—not his parents' bills, but the hungry eyes of a civet cat.

Before Harold could be seized, his parents flew at the cat, both roaring lustily and striking out with their great bills. In the ensuing mêlèe, Harold tumbled out of his nest and landed on our garden path.

Before the cat or any predator could get to him, Grandfather picked him up and took him to the sanctuary of the veranda.

Harold had lost some wing feathers and did not look as though he would be able to survive on his own, so we made an enclosure for him on our front veranda. Grandfather and I took over the duties of his parents.

Harold had a simple outlook, and once he had got over some early attacks of nerves, he began to welcome the approach of people. Grandfather and I meant the arrival of food and he greeted us with craning neck, quivering open bill, and a loud, croaking, '*Ka-ka-kaee!*'

Fruit, insect or animal food and green leaves were all welcome. We soon dispensed with the enclosure, but Harold made no effort to go away; he had difficulty flying. In fact, he asserted his tenancy rights, at least as far as the veranda was concerned.

One afternoon a veranda tea party was suddenly and alarmingly convulsed by a flash of black and white and noisy flapping. And behold, the last and only loaf of bread had been seized and carried off to his perch near the ceiling.

Harold was not beautiful by Hollywood standards. He had a small body and a large head. But he was good-natured and friendly, and he remained on good terms with most members of the household during his lifetime of twelve years.

Harold's best friends were those who fed him, and he was willing even to share his food with us, sometimes trying to feed me with his great beak.

While I turned down his offers of beetles and similar delicacies, I did occasionally share a banana with him. Eating was a serious business for Harold, and if there was any delay at mealtimes he would summon me with raucous barks and vigorous bangs of his bill on the woodwork of the kitchen window.

Having no family, profession or religion, Harold gave much time and thought to his personal appearance. He carried a rouge pot on his person and used it very skilfully as an item of his morning toilet.

This rouge pot was a small gland situated above the roots of his tail feathers; it produced a rich yellow fluid. Harold would dip into his rouge pot from time to time and then rub the colour over his feathers and the back of his neck. It would come off on my hands whenever I touched him.

Harold would toy with anything bright or glittering, often swallowing it afterwards.

He loved bananas and dates and balls of boiled rice. I would throw him the rice balls, and he would catch them in his beak, toss them in the air, and let them drop into his open mouth.

He perfected this trick of catching things, and in time I taught him to catch a tennis ball thrown with some force from a distance of fifteen yards. He would have made a great baseball catcher or an excellent slip fielder. On one occasion he seized a rupee coin from me (a week's pocket money in those days) and swallowed it neatly. Only once did he really misbehave. That was when he removed a lighted cigar from the hand of an American cousin who was visiting us. Harold swallowed the cigar. It was a moving experience for Harold, and an unnerving one for our guest.

Although Harold never seemed to drink any water, he loved the rain. We always knew when it was going to rain because Harold would start chuckling to himself about an hour before the first raindrops fell.

This used to irritate Aunt Ruby. She was always being caught in the rain. Harold would be chuckling when she left the house. And when she returned, drenched to the skin, he would be in fits of laughter.

As storm clouds would gather, and gusts of wind would shake the banana trees, Harold would get very excited, and his chuckle would change to an eerie whistle.

'*Wheee…wheee*,' he would scream, and then, as the first drops of rain hit the veranda steps, and the scent of the fresh earth passed through the house, he would start roaring with pleasure.

The wind would carry the rain into the veranda, and Harold would spread out his wings and dance, tumbling about like a circus clown. My grandparents and I would come out on the veranda and share his happiness.

Many years later, I still miss Harold's raucous bark and the banging of his great bill. If there is a heaven for good hornbills, I sincerely hope he is getting all the summer showers he could wish for, and plenty of tennis balls to catch.

Henry: A Chameleon

THIS IS the story of Henry, our pet chameleon. Chameleons are in a class by themselves and are no ordinary reptiles. They are easily distinguished from their nearest relatives, the lizards, by certain outstanding features. A chameleon's tongue is as long as its body. Its limbs are long and slender and its fingers and toes resemble a parrot's claws. On its head may be any of several ornaments. Henry had a rigid crest that looked like a fireman's helmet.

Henry's eyes were his most remarkable feature. They were not beautiful, but his left eye was quite independent of his right. He could move one eye without disturbing the other. Each eyeball, bulging out of his head, wobbled up and down, backward and forward. This frenzied movement gave Henry a horrible squint. And one look into Henry's frightful gaze was often enough to scare people into believing that chameleons are dangerous and poisonous reptiles.

One day, Grandfather was visiting a friend, when he came upon a noisy scene at the garden gate. Men were shouting, hurling stones, and brandishing sticks. The cause of the uproar was a chameleon that had been discovered sunning itself on a shrub. Someone claimed that the chameleon could poison people twenty feet away, simply by spitting at them. The residents of the area had risen up in arms. Grandfather was just in time to save the chameleon from certain death—he brought the little reptile home.

That chameleon was Henry, and that was how he came to live with us.

When I first visited Henry, he would treat me with great caution, sitting perfectly still on his perch with his back to me. The eye nearer to me would move around like the beam of a searchlight until it had me well in focus. Then it would stop and the other eye would begin an independent survey of its own. For a long time Henry trusted no one and responded to my friendliest gestures with grave suspicion.

Tiring of his wary attitude, I would tickle him gently in the ribs with my finger. This always threw him into a great rage. He would blow himself up to an enormous size as his lungs filled up with air, while his colour changed from green to red. He would sit up on his hind legs, swaying from side to side, hoping to overawe me. Opening his mouth very wide, he would let out an angry hiss. But his threatening display went no further. He did not bite.

Henry was a harmless fellow. If I put my finger in his mouth, even during his wildest moments, he would simply wait for me to take it out again. I suppose he could bite. His rigid jaws carried a number of finely pointed teeth. But Henry seemed convinced that his teeth were there for the sole purpose of chewing food, not fingers.

Henry was sometimes willing to take food from my hands. This he did very swiftly. His tongue performed like a boomerang and always came back to him with the food, usually an insect, attached to it.

Although Henry didn't cause any trouble in our house, he did create somewhat of a riot in the nursery down the road. It started out quite innocently.

When the papayas in our orchard were ripe, Grandmother sent a basketful to her friend Mrs Ghosh, who was the principal of the nursery school. While the basket sat waiting, Henry went searching for beetles and slipped in among the papayas, unnoticed. The gardener dutifully carried the basket to the school and left it in Mrs Ghosh's office. When Mrs Ghosh returned after making her rounds, she began examining and admiring the papayas. And out popped Henry.

Mrs Ghosh screamed. Henry squinted up at her, both eyes revolving furiously. Mrs Ghosh screamed again. Henry's colour changed from green to yellow to red. His mouth opened as though he, too, would like to scream. An assistant teacher rushed in, took one look at the chameleon, and joined in the shrieking.

Henry was terrified. He fled from the office, running down the corridor and into one of the classrooms. There he climbed up on a desk while children ran in all directions—some to get away from Henry, some to catch him. Henry finally made his exit through a window and disappeared in the garden.

Grandmother heard about the incident from Mrs Ghosh but didn't mention that the chameleon was ours. It might have spoiled their friendship.

Grandfather and I didn't think Henry would find his way back to us, because the school was three blocks away. But a few days later, I found him sunning himself on the garden wall. Although he looked none the worse for his adventure, he never went abroad again. Henry spent the rest of his days in the garden, where he kept the insect population well within bounds.

Monkey Trouble

GRANDFATHER BOUGHT Tutu from a street entertainer for the sum of ten rupees. The man had three monkeys. Tutu was the smallest, but the most mischievous. She was tied up most of the time. The little monkey looked so miserable with a collar and chain that Grandfather decided it would be much happier in our home. Grandfather had a weakness for keeping unusual pets. It was a habit that I, at the age of eight or nine, used to encourage.

Grandmother at first objected to having a monkey in the house. 'You have enough pets as it is,' she said, referring to Grandfather's goat, several white mice, and a small tortoise.

'But I don't have any,' I said.

'You're wicked enough for two monkeys. One boy in the house is all I can take.'

'Ah, but Tutu isn't a boy,' said Grandfather triumphantly. 'This is a little girl monkey!'

Grandmother gave in. She had always wanted a little girl in the house. She believed girls were less troublesome than boys. Tutu was to prove her wrong.

She was a pretty little monkey. Her bright eyes sparkled

with mischief beneath deep-set eyebrows. And her teeth, which were a pearly white, were often revealed in a grin that frightened the wits out of Aunt Ruby, whose nerves had already suffered from the presence of Grandfather's pet python. But this was my grandparents' house, and aunts and uncles had to put up with our pets.

Tutu's hands had a dried-up look, as though they had been pickled in the sun for many years. One of the first things I taught her was to shake hands, and this she insisted on doing with all who visited the house. Peppery Major Malik would have to stoop and shake hands with Tutu before he could enter the drawing room, otherwise Tutu would climb onto his shoulder and stay there, roughing up his hair and playing with his moustache.

Uncle Benji couldn't stand any of our pets and took a particular dislike to Tutu, who was always making faces at him. But as Uncle Benji was never in a job for long, and depended on Grandfather's good-natured generosity, he had to shake hands with Tutu, like everyone else.

Tutu's fingers were quick and wicked. And her tail, while adding to her good looks (Grandfather believed a tail would add to anyone's good looks!), also served as a third hand. She could use it to hang from a branch, and it was capable of scooping up any delicacy that might be out of reach of her hands.

On one of Aunt Ruby's visits, loud shrieks from her bedroom brought us running to see what was wrong. It was only Tutu trying on Aunt Ruby's petticoats! They were much too large, of course, and when Aunt Ruby entered the room, all she saw was a faceless white blob jumping up and down on the bed.

We disentangled Tutu and soothed Aunt Ruby. I gave Tutu a bunch of sweetpeas to make her happy. Granny didn't like anyone plucking her sweetpeas, so I took some from Major

Malik's garden while he was having his afternoon siesta.

Then Uncle Benji complained that his hairbrush was missing. We found Tutu sunning herself on the back veranda, using the hairbrush to scratch her armpits.

I took it from her and handed it back to Uncle Benji with an apology; but he flung the brush away with an oath.

'Such a fuss about nothing,' I said. 'Tutu doesn't have fleas!'

'No, and she bathes more often than Benji,' said Grandfather, who had borrowed Aunt Ruby's shampoo to give Tutu a bath.

All the same, Grandmother objected to Tutu being given the run of the house. Tutu had to spend her nights in the outhouse, in the company of the goat. They got on quite well, and it was not long before Tutu was seen sitting comfortably on the back of the goat, while the goat roamed the back garden in search of its favourite grass.

The day Grandfather had to visit Meerut to collect his railway pension, he decided to take Tutu and me along to keep us both out of mischief, he said. To prevent Tutu from wandering about on the train, causing inconvenience to passengers, she was provided with a large black travelling bag. This, with some straw at the bottom, became her compartment. Grandfather and I paid for our seats, and we took Tutu along as hand baggage.

There was enough space for Tutu to look out of the bag occasionally, and to be fed with bananas and biscuits, but she could not get her hands through the opening and the canvas was too strong for her to bite her way through.

Tutu's efforts to get out only had the effect of making the bag roll about on the floor or occasionally jump into the air—an exhibition that attracted a curious crowd of onlookers at the Dehra and Meerut railway stations.

Anyway, Tutu remained in the bag as far as Meerut, but while Grandfather was producing our tickets at the turnstile, she suddenly poked her head out of the bag and gave the ticket collector a wide grin.

The poor man was taken aback. But, with great presence of mind and much to Grandfather's annoyance, he said, 'Sir, you have a dog with you. You'll have to buy a ticket for it.'

'It's not a dog!' said Grandfather indignantly. 'This is a baby monkey of the species *Macacus mischievous*, closely related to the human species *Homus horriblis*! And there is no charge for babies!'

'It's as big as a cat,' said the ticket collector. 'Cats and dogs have to be paid for.'

'But, I tell you, it's only a baby!' protested Grandfather.

'Have you a birth certificate to prove that?' demanded the ticket collector.

'Next, you'll be asking to see her mother,' snapped Grandfather.

In vain did he take Tutu out of the bag. In vain did he try to prove that a young monkey did not qualify as a dog or a cat or even as a quadruped. Tutu was classified as a dog by the ticket collector, and five rupees were handed over as her fare.

Then Grandfather, just to get his own back, took from his pocket the small tortoise that he sometimes carried about, and said: 'And what must I pay for this, since you charge for all creatures great and small?'

The ticket collector looked closely at the tortoise, prodded it with his forefinger, gave Grandfather a triumphant look, and said, 'No charge, sir. It is not a dog!'

Winters in north India can be very cold. A great treat for Tutu on winter evenings was the large bowl of hot water given to her by Grandfather for a bath. Tutu would cunningly test the temperature with her hand, then gradually step into the bath, first one foot, then the other (as she had seen me doing) until she was in the water up to her neck.

Once comfortable, she would take the soap in her hands or feet and rub herself all over. When the water became cold, she would get out and run as quickly as she could to the kitchen fire in order to dry herself. If anyone laughed at her during this performance, Tutu's feelings would be hurt and she would refuse to go on with the bath.

One day Tutu almost succeeded in boiling herself alive. Grandmother had left a large kettle on the fire for tea. And Tutu, all by herself and with nothing better to do, decided to remove the lid. Finding the water just warm enough for a bath, she got in, with her head sticking out from the open kettle.

This was fine for a while, until the water began to get heated. Tutu raised herself a little. But finding it cold outside, she sat down again. She continued hopping up and down for some time, until Grandmother returned and hauled her, half-boiled, out of the kettle.

'What's for tea today?' asked Uncle Benji gleefully. 'Boiled eggs and a half-boiled monkey?'

But Tutu was none the worse for the adventure and continued to bathe more regularly than Uncle Benji.

Aunt Ruby was a frequent taker of baths. This met with Tutu's approval—so much so that, one day, when Aunt Ruby had finished shampooing her hair, she looked up through a lather of bubbles and soap suds to see Tutu sitting opposite her in the bath, following her example.

One day Aunt Ruby took us all by surprise. She announced that she had become engaged. We had always thought Aunt Ruby would never marry—she had often said so herself—but it appeared that the right man had now come along in the person of Rocky Fernandes, a schoolteacher from Goa.

Rocky was a tall, firm-jawed, good-natured man, a couple of

years younger than Aunt Ruby. He had a fine baritone voice and
sang in the manner of the great Nelson Eddy. As Grandmother
liked baritone singers, Rocky was soon in her good books.

'But what on earth does he see in her?' Uncle Benji wanted
to know.

'More than any girl has seen in you!' snapped Grandmother.
'Ruby's a fine girl. And they're both teachers. Maybe they can
start a school of their own.'

Rocky visited the house quite often and brought me
chocolates and cashew nuts, of which he seemed to have an
unlimited supply. He also taught me several marching songs.
Naturally, I approved of Rocky. Aunt Ruby won my grudging
admiration for having made such a wise choice.

One day I overheard them talking of going to the bazaar
to buy an engagement ring. I decided I would go along, too.
But as Aunt Ruby had made it clear that she did not want me
around, I decided that I had better follow at a discreet distance.
Tutu, becoming aware that a mission of some importance was
under way, decided to follow me. But as I had not invited her
along, she, too, decided to keep out of sight.

Once in the crowded bazaar, I was able to get quite close
to Aunt Ruby and Rocky without being spotted. I waited until
they had settled down in a large jewellery shop before sauntering
past and spotting them, as though by accident. Aunt Ruby
wasn't too pleased at seeing me, but Rocky waved and called
out, 'Come and join us! Help your aunt choose a beautiful ring!'

The whole thing seemed to be a waste of good money, but
I did not say so—Aunt Ruby was giving me one of her more
unloving looks.

'Look, these are pretty!' I said, pointing to some cheap,
bright agates set in white metal. But Aunt Ruby wasn't looking.
She was immersed in a case of diamonds.

'Why not a ruby for Aunt Ruby?' I suggested, trying to please her.

'That's her lucky stone,' said Rocky. 'Diamonds are the thing for engagements.' And he started singing a song about a diamond being a girl's best friend.

While the jeweller and Aunt Ruby were sifting through the diamond rings, and Rocky was trying out another tune, Tutu had slipped into the shop without being noticed by anyone but me. A little squeal of delight was the first sign she gave of her presence. Everyone looked up to see her trying on a pretty necklace.

'And what are those stones?' I asked.

'They look like pearls,' said Rocky.

'They *are* pearls,' said the shopkeeper, making a grab for them.

'It's that dreadful monkey!' cried Aunt Ruby. 'I knew that boy would bring him here!'

The necklace was already adorning Tutu's neck. I thought she looked rather nice in pearls, but she gave us no time to admire the effect. Springing out of our reach, Tutu dodged around Rocky, slipped between my legs, and made for the crowded road. I ran after her, shouting to her to stop, but she wasn't listening.

There were no branches to assist Tutu in her progress, but she used the heads and shoulders of people as springboards and so made rapid headway through the bazaar.

The jeweller left his shop and ran after us. So did Rocky. So did several bystanders who had seen the incident. And others, who had no idea what it was all about, joined in the chase. As Grandfather used to say, 'In a crowd, everyone plays follow-the-leader, even when they don't know who's leading.' Not everyone knew that the leader was Tutu. Only the front runners could see her.

She tried to make her escape speedier by leaping onto the back of a passing scooterist. The scooter swerved into a fruit stall and came to a standstill under a heap of bananas, while the scooterist found himself in the arms of an indignant fruitseller. Tutu peeled a banana and ate part of it, before deciding to move on.

From an awning, she made an emergency landing on a washerman's donkey. The donkey promptly panicked and rushed down the road, while bundles of washing fell by the wayside. The washerman joined in the chase. Children on their way to school decided that there was something better to do than attend classes. With shouts of glee, they soon overtook their panting elders.

Tutu finally left the bazaar and took a road leading in the direction of our house. But knowing that she would be caught and locked up once she got home, she decided to end the chase by ridding herself of the necklace. Deftly removing it from her neck, she flung it in the small canal that ran down the road.

The jeweller, with a cry of anguish, plunged into the canal. So did Rocky. So did I. So did several other people, both adults and children. It was to be a treasure hunt!

Some twenty minutes later, Rocky shouted, 'I've found it!' Covered in mud, waterlilies, ferns and tadpoles, we emerged from the canal, and Rocky presented the necklace to the relieved shopkeeper.

Everyone trudged back to the bazaar to find Aunt Ruby waiting in the shop, still trying to make up her mind about a suitable engagement ring.

Finally the ring was bought, the engagement was announced, and a date was set for the wedding.

'I don't want that monkey anywhere near us on our wedding

day,' declared Aunt Ruby.

'We'll lock her up in the outhouse,' promised Grandfather. 'And we'll let her out only after you've left for your honeymoon.'

A few days before the wedding I found Tutu in the kitchen, helping Grandmother prepare the wedding cake. Tutu often helped with the cooking and, when Grandmother wasn't looking, added herbs, spices and other interesting items to the pots—so that occasionally we found a chilli in the custard or an onion in the jelly or a strawberry floating in the chicken soup.

Sometimes these additions improved a dish, sometimes they did not. Uncle Benji lost a tooth when he bit firmly into a sandwich which contained walnut shells.

I'm not sure exactly what went into that wedding cake when Grandmother wasn't looking—she insisted that Tutu was always very well-behaved in the kitchen—but I did spot Tutu stirring in some red chilli sauce, bitter gourd seeds, and a generous helping of egg shells!

It's true that some of the guests were not seen for several days after the wedding, but no one said anything against the cake. Most people thought it had an interesting flavour.

The great day dawned, and the wedding guests made their way to the little church that stood on the outskirts of Dehra—a town with a church, two mosques, and several temples.

I had offered to dress Tutu up as a bridesmaid and bring her along, but no one except Grandfather thought it was a good idea. So I was an obedient boy and locked Tutu in the outhouse. I did, however, leave the skylight open a little. Grandmother had always said that fresh air was good for growing children, and I thought Tutu should have her share of it.

The wedding ceremony went without a hitch. Aunt Ruby looked a picture, and Rocky looked like a film star.

Grandfather played the organ, and did so with such gusto

that the small choir could hardly be heard. Grandmother cried a little. I sat quietly in a corner, with the little tortoise on my lap.

When the service was over, we trooped out into the sunshine and made our way back to the house for the reception.

The feast had been laid out on tables in the garden. As the gardener had been left in charge, everything was in order. Tutu was on her best behaviour. She had, it appeared, used the skylight to avail of more fresh air outside, and now sat beside the three-tier wedding cake, guarding it against crows, squirrels and the goat. She greeted the guests with squeals of delight.

It was too much for Aunt Ruby. She flew at Tutu in a rage. And Tutu, sensing that she was not welcome, leapt away, taking with her the top tier of the wedding cake.

Led by Major Malik, we followed her into the orchard, only to find that she had climbed to the top of the jackfruit tree. From there she proceeded to pelt us with bits of wedding cake. She had also managed to get hold of a bag of confetti, and when she ran out of cake she showered us with confetti.

'That's more like it!' said the good-humoured Rocky. 'Now let's return to the party, folks!'

Uncle Benji remained with Major Malik, determined to chase Tutu away. He kept throwing stones into the tree, until he received a large piece of cake bang on his nose. Muttering threats, he returned to the party, leaving the major to do battle.

When the festivities were finally over, Uncle Benji took the old car out of the garage and drove up the veranda steps. He was going to drive Aunt Ruby and Rocky to the nearby hill resort of Mussoorie, where they would have their honeymoon.

Watched by family and friends, Aunt Ruby climbed into the back seat. She waved regally to everyone. She leant out of the window and offered me her cheek and I had to kiss her farewell. Everyone wished them luck.

As Rocky burst into song, Uncle Benji opened the throttle and stepped on the accelerator. The car shot forward in a cloud of dust.

Rocky and Aunt Ruby continued to wave to us. And so did Tutu, from her perch on the rear bumper! She was clutching a bag in her hands and showering confetti on all who stood in the driveway.

'They don't know Tutu's with them!' I exclaimed. 'She'll go all the way to Mussoorie! Will Aunt Ruby let her stay with them?'

'Tutu might ruin the honeymoon,' said Grandfather. 'But don't worry—our Benji will bring her back!'

Snake Trouble

1

AFTER RETIRING from the Indian Railways and settling in Dehra, Grandfather often made his days (and ours) more exciting by keeping unusual pets. He paid a snake charmer in the bazaar twenty rupees for a young python. Then, to the delight of a curious group of boys and girls, he slung the python over his shoulder and brought it home.

I was with him at the time, and felt very proud walking beside Grandfather. He was popular in Dehra, especially among the poorer people, and everyone greeted him politely without seeming to notice the python. They were, in fact, quite used to seeing him in the company of strange creatures.

The first to see us arrive was Tutu the monkey, who was swinging from a branch of the jackfruit tree. One look at the python, ancient enemy of her race, and she fled into the house squealing with fright. Then our parrot, Popeye, who had his perch on the veranda, set up the most awful shrieking and whistling. His whistle was like that of a steam engine. He had learnt to do this in earlier days, when we had lived near railway stations.

The noise brought Grandmother to the veranda, where she nearly fainted at the sight of the python curled round Grandfather's neck.

Grandmother put up with most of his pets, but she drew the line at reptiles. Even a sweet-tempered lizard made her blood run cold. There was little chance that she would allow a python in the house.

'It will strangle you to death!' she cried.

'Nonsense,' said Grandfather. 'He's only a young fellow.'

'He'll soon get used to us,' I added by way of support.

'He might, indeed,' said Grandmother, 'but I have no intention of getting used to him. And your Aunt Ruby is coming to stay with us tomorrow. She'll leave the minute she knows there's a snake in the house.'

'Well, perhaps we should show it to her first thing,' said Grandfather, who found Aunt Ruby rather tiresome.

'Get rid of it right away,' said Grandmother.

'I can't let it loose in the garden. It might find its way into the chicken shed, and then where will we be?'

'Minus a few chickens,' I said reasonably, but this only made Grandmother more determined to get rid of the python.

'Lock that awful thing in the bathroom,' she said. 'Go and find the man you bought it from, and get him to come here and collect it! He can keep the money you gave him.'

Grandfather and I took the snake into the bathroom and placed it in an empty tub. Looking a bit crestfallen, he said, 'Perhaps your grandmother is right. I'm not worried about Aunt Ruby, but we don't want the python to get hold of Tutu or Popeye.'

We hurried off to the bazaar in search of the snake charmer

but hadn't gone far when we found several snake charmers looking for us. They had heard that Grandfather was buying snakes, and they had brought with them snakes of various sizes and descriptions.

'No, no!' protested Grandfather. 'We don't want more snakes. We want to return the one we bought.'

But the man who had sold it to us had, apparently, returned to his village in the jungle, looking for another python for Grandfather; and the other snake charmers were not interested in buying, only in selling. In order to shake them off, we had to return home by a roundabout route, climbing a wall and cutting through an orchard. We found Grandmother pacing up and down the veranda. One look at our faces and she knew we had failed to get rid of the snake.

'All right,' said Grandmother. 'Just take it away yourselves and see that it doesn't come back.'

'We'll get rid of it, Grandmother,' I said confidently. 'Don't you worry.'

Grandfather opened the bathroom door and stepped into the room. I was close behind him. We couldn't see the python anywhere.

'He's gone,' announced Grandfather.

'We left the window open,' I said.

'Deliberately, no doubt,' said Grandmother. 'But it couldn't have gone far. You'll have to search the grounds.'

A careful search was made of the house, the roof, the kitchen, the garden and the chicken shed, but there was no sign of the python.

'He must have gone over the garden wall,' Grandfather said cheerfully. 'He'll be well away by now!'

The python did not reappear, and when Aunt Ruby arrived with enough luggage to show that she had come for a long visit, there was only the parrot to greet her with a series of long, ear-splitting whistles.

2

For a couple of days Grandfather and I were a little worried that the python might make a sudden reappearance, but when he didn't show up again, we felt he had gone for good. Aunt Ruby had to put up with Tutu the monkey making faces at her, something I did only when she wasn't looking; and she complained that Popeye shrieked loudest when she was in the room; but she was used to them, and knew she would have to bear with them if she was going to stay with us.

And then, one evening, we were startled by a scream from the garden.

Seconds later, Aunt Ruby came flying up the veranda steps, gasping, 'In the guava tree! I was reaching for a guava when I saw it staring at me. The look in its eyes! As though it would eat me alive—'

'Calm down, dear,' urged Grandmother, sprinkling rose water over my aunt. 'Tell us, what *did* you see?'

'A snake!' sobbed Aunt Ruby. 'A great boa constrictor in the guava tree. Its eyes were terrible, and it looked at me in such a queer way.'

'Trying to tempt you with a guava, no doubt,' said Grandfather, turning away to hide his smile. He gave me a look full of meaning, and I hurried out into the garden. But when I got to the guava tree, the python (if it had been the python) had gone.

'Aunt Ruby must have frightened it off,' I told Grandfather.

'I'm not surprised,' he said. 'But it will be back, Ranji. I think it has taken a fancy to your aunt.'

Sure enough, the python began to make brief but frequent appearances, usually up in the most unexpected places.

One morning I found him curled up on a dressing table, gazing at his own reflection in the mirror. I went for Grandfather, but by the time we returned the python had moved on.

He was seen again in the garden, and one day I spotted him climbing the iron ladder to the roof. I set off after him, and was soon up the ladder, which I had climbed up many times. I arrived on the flat roof just in time to see the snake disappearing down a drainpipe. The end of his tail was visible for a few moments and then that, too, disappeared.

'I think he lives in the drainpipe,' I told Grandfather.

'Where does it get its food?' asked Grandmother.

'Probably lives on those field rats that used to be such a nuisance. Remember, they lived in the drainpipes, too.'

'Hmm…' Grandmother looked thoughtful. 'A snake has its uses. Well, as long as it keeps to the roof and prefers rats to chickens…'

But the python did not confine itself to the roof. Piercing shrieks from Aunt Ruby had us all rushing to her room. There was the python on *her* dressing table, apparently admiring himself in the mirror.

'All the attention he's been getting has probably made him conceited,' said Grandfather, picking up the python to the accompaniment of further shrieks from Aunt Ruby. 'Would you like to hold him for a minute, Ruby? He seems to have taken a fancy to you.'

Aunt Ruby ran from the room and onto the veranda, where she was greeted with whistles of derision from Popeye the parrot. Poor Aunt Ruby! She cut short her stay by a week and returned to Lucknow, where she was a schoolteacher. She said she felt safer in her school than she did in our house.

3

Having seen Grandfather handle the python with such ease and confidence, I decided I would do likewise. So the next time I saw the snake climbing the ladder to the roof, I climbed up alongside him. He stopped, and I stopped too. I put out my hand, and he slid over my arm and up to my shoulder. As I did not want him coiling round my neck, I gripped him with both hands and carried him down to the garden. He didn't seem to mind.

The snake felt rather cold and slippery and at first he gave me goose pimples. But I soon got used to him, and he must have liked the way I handled him, because when I set him down he wanted to climb up my leg. As I had other things to do, I dropped him in a large empty basket that had been left out in the garden. He stared out at me with unblinking, expressionless eyes. There was no way of knowing what he was thinking, if indeed he thought at all.

I went off for a bicycle ride, and when I returned, I found Grandmother picking guavas and dropping them into the basket. The python must have gone elsewhere.

When the basket was full, Grandmother said, 'Will you take these over to Major Malik? It's his birthday and I want to give him a nice surprise.'

I fixed the basket on the carrier of my cycle and pedalled off to Major Malik's house at the end of the road. The major met me on the steps of his house.

'And what has your kind granny sent me today, Ranji?' he asked.

'A surprise for your birthday, sir,' I said, and put the basket down in front of him.

The python, who had been buried beneath all the guavas,

chose this moment to wake up and stand straight up to a height of several feet. Guavas tumbled all over the place. The major uttered an oath and dashed indoors.

I pushed the python back into the basket, picked it up, mounted the bicycle, and rode out of the gate in record time. And it was as well that I did so, because Major Malik came charging out of the house armed with a double-barrelled shotgun, which he was waving all over the place.

'Did you deliver the guavas?' asked Grandmother when I got back.

'I delivered them,' I said truthfully.

'And was he pleased?'

'He's going to write and thank you,' I said.

And he did.

'*Thank you for the lovely surprise,*' he wrote. '*Obviously you could not have known that my doctor had advised me against any undue excitement. My blood pressure has been rather high. The sight of your grandson does not improve it. All the same, it's the thought that matters and I take it all in good humour...*'

'What a strange letter,' said Grandmother. 'He must be ill, poor man. Are guavas bad for blood pressure?'

'Not by themselves, they aren't,' said Grandfather, who had an inkling of what had happened. 'But together with other things they can be a bit upsetting.'

4

Just when all of us, including Grandmother, were getting used to having the python about the house and grounds, it was decided that we would be going to Lucknow for a few months.

Lucknow was a large city, about three hundred miles from Dehra. Aunt Ruby lived and worked there. We would be staying with her, and so, of course, we couldn't take any pythons, monkeys or other unusual pets with us.

'What about Popeye?' I asked.

'Popeye isn't a pet,' said Grandmother. 'He's one of us. He comes too.'

And so the Dehra railway platform was thrown into confusion by the shrieks and whistles of our parrot, who could imitate both the guard's whistle and the whistle of a train. People dashed into their compartments, thinking the train was about to leave, only to realize that the guard hadn't blown his whistle after all. When they got down, Popeye would let out another shrill whistle, which sent everyone rushing for the train again. This happened several times until the guard actually blew his whistle. Then nobody bothered to get on, and several passengers were left behind.

'Can't you gag that parrot?' asked Grandfather, as the train moved out of the station and picked up speed.

'I'll do nothing of the sort,' said Grandmother. 'I've bought a ticket for him, and he's entitled to enjoy the journey as much as anyone.'

Whenever we stopped at a station, Popeye objected to fruit sellers and other people poking their heads in through the windows. Before the journey was over, he had nipped two fingers and a nose, and tweaked a ticket inspector's ear.

It was to be a night journey, and, presently, Grandmother covered herself with a blanket and stretched out on the berth. 'It's been a tiring day. I think I'll go to sleep,' she said.

'Aren't we going to eat anything?' I asked.

'I'm not hungry—I had something before we left the house. You two help yourselves from the picnic hamper.'

Grandmother dozed off, and even Popeye started nodding, lulled to sleep by the clackety-clack of the wheels and the steady puffing of the steam engine.

'Well, I'm hungry,' I said. 'What did Granny make for us?'

'Stuffed samosas, omelettes, and tandoori chicken. It's all in the hamper under the berth.

I tugged at the cane box and dragged it into the middle of the compartment. The straps were loosely tied. No sooner had I undone them than the lid flew open, and I let out a gasp of surprise.

In the hamper was a python, curled up contentedly. There was no sign of our dinner.

'It's a python,' I said. 'And it's finished all our dinner.'

'Nonsense,' said Grandfather, joining me near the hamper. 'Pythons won't eat omelettes and samosas. They like their food alive! Why, this isn't our hamper. The one with our food in it must have been left behind! Wasn't it Major Malik who helped us with our luggage? I think he's got his own back on us by changing the hamper!'

Grandfather snapped the hamper shut and pushed it back beneath the berth.

'Don't let Grandmother see him,' he said. 'She might think we brought him along on purpose.'

'Well, I'm hungry,' I complained.

'Wait till we get to the next station, then we can buy some pakoras. Meanwhile, try some of Popeye's green chillies.'

'No thanks,' I said. 'You have them, Grandad.'

And Grandfather, who could eat chillies plain, popped a couple into his mouth and munched away contentedly.

A little after midnight there was a great clamour at the end of the corridor. Popeye made complaining squawks, and Grandfather and I got up to see what was wrong.

Suddenly there were cries of 'Snake, snake!'

I looked under the berth. The hamper was open.

'The python's out,' I said, and Grandfather dashed out of the compartment in his pyjamas. I was close behind.

About a dozen passengers were bunched together outside the washroom.

'Anything wrong?' asked Grandfather casually.

'We can't get into the toilet,' said someone. 'There's a huge snake inside.'

'Let me take a look,' said Grandfather. 'I know all about snakes.'

The passengers made way, and Grandfather and I entered the washroom together, but there was no sign of the python.

'He must have got out through the ventilator,' said Grandfather. 'By now he'll be in another compartment!' Emerging from the washroom, he told the assembled passengers, 'It's gone! Nothing to worry about. Just a harmless young python.'

When we got back to our compartment, Grandmother was sitting up on her berth.

'I *knew* you'd do something foolish behind my back,' she scolded. 'You told me you'd left that creature behind, and all the time it was with us on the train.'

Grandfather tried to explain that we had nothing to do with it, that this python had been smuggled onto the train by Major Malik, but Grandmother was unconvinced.

'Anyway, it's gone,' said Grandfather. 'It must have fallen out of the washroom window. We're over a hundred miles from Dehra, so you'll never see it again.'

Even as he spoke, the train slowed down and lurched to a grinding halt.

'No station here,' said Grandfather, putting his head out of the window.

Someone came rushing along the embankment, waving his arms and shouting.

'I do believe it's the stoker,' said Grandfather. 'I'd better go and see what's wrong.'

'I'm coming too,' I said, and together we hurried along the length of the stationary train until we reached the engine.

'What's up?' called Grandfather. 'Anything I can do to help? I know all about engines.'

But the engine driver was speechless. And who could blame him? The python had curled itself about his legs, and the driver was too petrified to move.

'Just leave it to us,' said Grandfather, and, dragging the python off the driver, he dumped the snake in my arms. The engine driver sank down on the floor, pale and trembling.

'I think I'd better drive the engine,' said Grandfather. 'We don't want to be late getting into Lucknow. Your aunt will be expecting us!' And before the astonished driver could protest, Grandfather had released the brakes and set the engine in motion.

'We've left the stoker behind,' I said.

'Never mind. You can shovel the coal.'

Only too glad to help Grandfather drive an engine, I dropped the python in the driver's lap and started shovelling coal. The engine picked up speed and we were soon rushing through the darkness, sparks flying skywards and the steam whistle shrieking almost without pause.

'You're going too fast!' cried the driver.

'Making up for lost time,' said Grandfather. 'Why did the stoker run away?'

'He went for the guard. You've left them both behind!'

5

Early next morning, the train steamed safely into Lucknow. Explanations were in order, but as the Lucknow station master was an old friend of Grandfather's, all was well. We had arrived twenty minutes early, and while Grandfather went off to have a cup of tea with the engine driver and the station master, I returned the python to the hamper and helped Grandmother with the luggage. Popeye stayed perched on Grandmother's shoulder, eyeing the busy platform with deep distrust. He was the first to see Aunt Ruby striding down the platform, and let out a warning whistle.

Aunt Ruby, a lover of good food, immediately spotted the picnic hamper, picked it up and said, 'It's quite heavy. You must have kept something for me! I'll carry it out to the taxi.'

'We hardly ate anything,' I said.

'It seems ages since I tasted something cooked by your granny.' And after that there was no getting the hamper away from Aunt Ruby.

Glancing at it, I thought I saw the lid bulging, but I had tied it down quite firmly this time and there was little likelihood of its suddenly bursting open.

Grandfather joined us outside the station and we were soon settled inside the taxi. Aunt Ruby gave instructions to the driver and we shot off in a cloud of dust.

'I'm dying to see what's in the hamper,' said Aunt Ruby. 'Can't I take just a little peek?'

'Not now,' said Grandfather. 'First let's enjoy the breakfast you've got waiting for us.'

Popeye, perched proudly on Grandmother's shoulder, kept one suspicious eye on the quivering hamper.

When we got to Aunt Ruby's house, we found breakfast laid out on the dining table.

'It isn't much,' said Aunt Ruby. 'But we'll supplement it with what you've brought in the hamper.'

Placing the hamper on the table, she lifted the lid and

peered inside. And promptly fainted.

Grandfather picked up the python, took it into the garden, and draped it over a branch of a pomegranate tree.

When Aunt Ruby recovered, she insisted that she had seen a huge snake in the picnic hamper. We showed her the empty basket.

'You're seeing things,' said Grandfather. 'You've been working too hard.'

'Teaching is a very tiring job,' I said solemnly.

Grandmother said nothing. But Popeye broke into loud squawks and whistles, and soon everyone, including a slightly hysterical Aunt Ruby, was doubled up with laughter.

But the snake must have tired of the joke because we never saw it again!

The Eyes of the Eagle

It was a high, piercing sound, almost like the yelping of a dog. Jai stopped picking the wild strawberries that grew in the grass around him, and looked up at the sky. He had a dog—a shaggy guard-dog called Motu—but Motu did not yet yelp, he growled and barked. The strange sound came from the sky, and Jai had heard it before. Now, realizing what it was, he jumped to his feet, calling to his dog, calling his sheep to start for home. Motu came bounding towards him, ready for a game.

'Not now, Motu!' said Jai. 'We must get the lambs home quickly.' Again he looked up at the sky.

He saw it now, a black speck against the sun, growing larger as it circled the mountain, coming lower every moment—a golden eagle, king of the skies over the higher Himalayas, ready now to swoop and seize its prey.

Had it seen a pheasant or a pine marten? Or was it after one of the lambs? Jai had never lost a lamb to an eagle, but recently some of the other shepherds had been talking about a golden eagle that had been preying on their flocks.

The sheep had wandered some way down the side of the mountain, and Jai ran after them to make sure that none of the lambs had gone off on its own.

Motu ran about, barking furiously. He wasn't very good at keeping the sheep together—he was often bumping into then and sending them tumbling down the slope—but his size and bear-like look kept the leopards and wolves at a distance.

Jai was counting the lambs; they were bleating loudly and staying close to their mothers. *One—two—three—four...*

There should have been a fifth. Jai couldn't see it on the slope below him. He looked up towards a rocky ledge near the steep path to the Tung temple. The golden eagle was circling the rocks.

The bird disappeared from sight for a moment, then rose again with a small creature grasped firmly in its terrible talons.

'It has taken a lamb!' shouted Jai. He started scrambling up the slope. Motu ran ahead of him, barking furiously at the big bird as it glided away, over the tops of the stunted junipers to its eyrie on the cliffs above Tung.

There was nothing that Jai and Motu could do except stare helplessly and angrily at the disappearing eagle. The lamb had died the instant it had been struck. The rest of the flock seemed unaware of what had happened. They still grazed on the thick, sweet grass of the mountain slopes.

'We had better drive them home, Motu,' said Jai, and at a nod from the boy, the big dog bounded down the slope, to take part in his favourite game of driving the sheep homewards. Soon he had them running all over the place, and Jai had to dash about trying to keep them together. Finally, they straggled homewards.

A fine lamb gone,' said Jai to himself gloomily. 'I wonder what Grandfather will say'

Grandfather said, 'Never mind. It had to happen some day. That eagle has been watching the sheep for some time.'

Grandmother, more practical, said; 'We could have sold the lamb for three hundred rupees. You'll have to be more careful in future, Jai. Don't fall asleep on the hillside, and don't read story-books when you are supposed to be watching the sheep!'

'I wasn't reading this morning,' said Jai truthfully, forgetting to mention that he had been gathering strawberries.

'It's good for him to read,' said Grandfather, who had never had the luck to go to school. In his days, there weren't any schools in the mountains. Now there was one in every village.

'Time enough to read at night,' said Grandmother, who did not think much of the little one-room school down at Maku, their home village.

'Well, these are the October holidays,' said Grandfather. 'Otherwise he would not be here to help us with the sheep. It will snow by the end of the month, and then we will move with the flock. You will have more time for reading then, Jai.'

At Maku, which was down in the warmer valley, Jai's parents tilled a few narrow terraces on which they grew barley, millets and potatoes. The old people brought their sheep up to the Tung meadows to graze during the summer months. They stayed in a small stone hut just off the path which pilgrims took to the ancient temple. At 12,000 feet above sea level, it was the highest Hindu temple on the inner Himalayan ranges.

The following day Jai and Motu were very careful. The did not let the sheep out of sight even for a minute. Nor did they catch sight of the golden eagle. 'What if it attacks again?' wondered Jai. 'How will I stop it?'

The great eagle, with its powerful beak and talons, was more than a match for boy or dog. Its hind claw, four inches round the curve, was its most dangerous weapon. When it spread its wings, the distance from tip to tip was more than eight feet

The eagle did not come that day because it had fed well and

was now resting in its eyrie. Old bones, which had belonged to pheasants, snow-cocks, pine martens and even foxes, were scattered about the rocks which formed the eagle's home. The eagle had a mate, but it was not the breeding season and she was away on a scouting expedition of her own.

The golden eagle stood on its rocky ledge, staring majestically across the valley. Its hard, unblinking eyes missed nothing. Those strange orange-yellow eyes could spot a field rat or a mouse hare more than a hundred yards below.

There were other eagles on the mountain, but usually they kept to their own territory. And only the bolder ones went for lambs, because the flocks were always protected by men and dogs.

The eagle took off from its eyrie and glided gracefully, powerfully over the valley, circling the Tung mountain.

Below lay the old temple, built from slabs of grey granite. A line of pilgrims snaked up the steep, narrow path. On the meadows below the peak, the sheep grazed peacefully, unaware of the presence of the eagle. The great bird's shadow slid over the sunlit slopes.

The eagle saw the boy and the dog, but he did not fear them. He had his eye on a lamb that was frisking about on the grass, a few feet away from the other grazing sheep.

Jai did not see the eagle until it swept round an outcrop of rocks about a hundred feet away. It moved silently, without any movement of its wings, for it had already built up the momentum for its dive. Now it came straight at the lamb.

Motu saw the bird in time. With a low growl he dashed forward and reached the side of the lamb at almost the same instant that the eagle swept in.

There was a terrific collision. Feathers flew. The eagle screamed with rage. The lamb tumbled down the slope, and Motu howled in pain as the huge beak struck him high on the leg.

The big bird, a little stunned by the clash, flew off rather unsteadily, with a mighty beating of its wings.

Motu had saved the lamb. It was frightened but unhurt. Bleating loudly, it joined the other sheep, who took up the bleating. Jai ran up to Motu, who lay whimpering on the ground. There was no sign of the eagle. Quickly he removed his shirt and vest; then he wrapped his vest round the dog's wound, tying it in position with his belt.

Motu could not get up, and he was much too heavy for Jai to carry. Jai did not want to leave his dog alone, in case the eagle returned to attack.

He stood up, cupped his hand to his mouth, and began calling for his grandfather.

'Dada, dada!' he shouted, and presently Grandfather heard him and came stumbling down the slope. He was followed by another shepherd, and together they lifted Motu and carried him home.

Motu had a bad wound, but Grandmother cleaned it and applied a paste made of herbs. Then she laid strips of carrot over the wound—an old mountain remedy—and bandaged the leg. But it would be some time before Motu could run about again By then it would probably be snowing and time to leave these high-altitude pastures and return to the valley. Meanwhile, the sheep had to be taken out to graze, and Grandfather decided to accompany Jai for the remaining period.

They did not see the golden eagle for two or three days, and, when they did, it was flying over the next range. Perhaps it had found some other source of food, or even another flock of sheep 'Are you afraid of the eagle?' Grandfather asked Jai.

'I wasn't before,' said Jai. 'Not until it hurt Motu. I did not know it could be so dangerous. But Motu hurt it too. He banged straight into it!'

'Perhaps it won't bother us again,' said Grandfather thoughtfully. 'A bird's wing is easily injured—even an eagle's.'

Jai wasn't so sure. He had seen it strike twice, and he knew that it was not afraid of anyone. Only when it learnt to fear his presence would it keep away from the flock.

The next day Grandfather did not feel well; he was feverish and kept to his bed. Motu was hobbling about gamely on three legs; the wounded leg was still very sore.

'Don't go too far with the sheep,' said Grandmother. 'Let them graze near the house.'

'But there's hardly any grass here,' said Jai.

'I don't want you wandering off while that eagle is still around.'

'Give him my stick,' said Grandfather from his bed. Grandmother took it from the corner and handed it to the boy.

It was an old stick, made of wild cherry wood, which Grandfather often carried around. The wood was strong and well-seasoned; the stick was stout and long. It reached up to Jai's shoulders.

'Don't lose it,' said Grandfather. 'It was given to me many years ago by a wandering scholar who came to the Tung temple. I was going to give it to you when you got bigger, but perhaps this is the right time for you to have it. If the eagle comes near you, swing the stick around your head. That should frighten it off.'

Clouds had gathered over the mountains, and a heavy mist hid the Tung temple. With the approach of winter, the flow of pilgrims had been reduced to a trickle. The shepherds had started leaving the lush meadows and returning to their villages at lower altitudes. Very soon, the bears and the leopards and the golden eagles would have the high ranges all to themselves.

Jai used the cherry wood stick to prod the sheep along the

path until they reached the steep meadows. The stick would have to be a substitute for Motu. And they seemed to respond to it more readily than they did to Motu's mad charges.

Because of the sudden cold and the prospect of snow, Grandmother had made Jai wear a rough woollen jacket and a pair of high boots bought from a Tibetan trader. He wasn't used to the boots—he wore sandals at other times—and had some difficulty in climbing quickly up and down the hillside. It was tiring work, trying to keep the flock together. The cawing of some crows warned Jai that the eagle might be around, but the mist prevented him from seeing very far.

After some time the mist lifted and Jai was able to see the temple and the snow-peaks towering behind it. He saw the golden eagle, too. It was circling high overhead. Jai kept close to the flock—one eye on the eagle, one eye on the restless sheep.

Then the great bird stooped and flew lower. It circled the temple and then pretended to go away. Jai felt sure it would be back. And a few minutes later, it reappeared from the other side of the mountain. It was much lower now, wings spread out and back, taloned feet to the fore, piercing eyes fixed on its target—a small lamb that had suddenly gone frisking down the slope, away from Jai and the flock.

Now it flew lower still, only a few feet off the ground, paying no attention to the boy.

It passed Jai with a great rush of air, and, as it did so, the boy struck out with his stick and caught the bird a glancing blow.

The eagle missed its prey, and the tiny lamb skipped away.

To Jai's amazement, the bird did not fly off. Instead it landed on the hillside and glared at the boy, as a king would glare at a humble subject who had dared to pelt him with a pebble.

The golden eagle stood almost as tall as Jai. Its wings were still outspread. Its fierce eyes seemed to be looking through and through the boy.

Jai's first instinct was to turn and run. But the cherry wood stick was still in his hands, and he felt sure there was power in it. He saw that the eagle was about to launch itself again at the lamb. Instead of running away, he ran forward, the stick raised above his head.

The eagle rose a few feet off the ground and struck out with its huge claws.

Luckily for Jai, his heavy jacket took the force of the blow. A talon ripped through the sleeve, and the sleeve fell away. At the same time the heavy stick caught the eagle across its open wing. The bird gave a shrill cry of pain and fury. Then it turned and flapped heavily away, flying unsteadily because of its injured wing.

Jai still clutched the stick, because he expected the bird to return; he did not even glance at his torn jacket. But the golden eagle had alighted on a distant rock and was in no hurry to return to the attack.

Jai began driving the sheep home. The clouds had become heavy and black, and presently the first snow-flakes began to fall.

Jai saw a hare go lolloping down the hill. When it was about fifty yards away, there was a rush of air from the eagle's beating wings, and Jai saw the bird approaching the hare in a sidelong drive.

'So it hasn't been badly hurt,' thought Jai, feeling a little relieved, for he could not help admiring the great bird. 'Now it has found something else to chase for its dinner.'

The hare saw the eagle and dodged about, making for a clump of junipers. Jai did not know if it was caught or not, because the snow and sleet had increased and both bird and hare were lost in the gathering snow-storm.

The sheep were bleating behind him. One of the lambs looked tired, and he stooped to pick it up. As he did so, he heard a thin, whining sound. It grew louder by the second. Before he could look up, a huge wing caught him across the shoulders and sent him sprawling. The lamb tumbled down the slope with him, into a thorny bilberry bush.

The bush saved them. Jai saw the eagle coming in again, flying low. It was another eagle! One had been vanquished, and now here was another, just as big and fearless, probably the mate of the first eagle.

Jai had lost his stick and there was no way by which he could fight the second eagle. So he crept further into the bush, holding the lamb beneath him. At the same time he began shouting at the top of his voice—both to scare the bird away and to summon help. The eagle could not easily get at them now; but the rest of the flock was exposed on the hillside. Surely the eagle would make for them.

Even as the bird circled and came back in another dive, Jai heard fierce barking. The eagle immediately swung away and rose skywards.

The barking came from Motu. Hearing Jai's shouts and sensing that something was wrong, he had come limping out of the house, ready to do battle. Behind him came another shepherd and—most wonderful of all—Grandmother herself, banging two frying-pans together. The barking, the banging and the shouting frightened the eagles away. The sheep scattered too, and it was some time before they could all be rounded up. By then it was snowing heavily.

'Tomorrow we must all go down to Maku,' said the shepherd.

'Yes, it's time we went,' said Grandmother. 'You can read your story-books again, Jai.'

'I'll have my own story to tell,' said Jai.

When they reached the hut and Jai saw Grandfather, he said, 'Oh, I've forgotten your stick!'

But Motu had picked it up. Carrying it between his teeth, he brought it home and sat down with it in the open doorway. He had decided the cherry wood was good for his teeth and would have chewed it up if Grandmother hadn't taken it from him.

'Never mind,' said Grandfather, sitting up on his cot. 'It isn't the stick that matters. It's the person who holds it.'

The Parrot Who Wouldn't Talk

'You're no beauty! Can't talk, can't sing, can't dance!'

With these words Aunt Ruby would taunt the unfortunate parakeet who glared morosely at everyone from his ornamental cage at one end of the long veranda of Granny's bungalow in north India.

In those distant days, almost everyone—Indian or European—kept a pet parrot or parakeet, or 'lovebird' as some of the smaller ones were called. Sometimes these birds became great talkers, or rather mimics, and would learn to recite entire mantras (religious chants), or admonitions to the children of the house, such as *'Paro, beta, paro!'* ('Study, child, study!') or, for the benefit of boys like me—'Don't be greedy, don't be greedy.'

These expressions were, of course, picked up by the parrot over a period of time, after many repetitions by whichever member of the household had taken on the task of teaching the bird to talk.

But our parrot refused to talk.

He'd been bought by Aunt Ruby from a birdcatcher who'd visited all the houses on our road, selling caged birds ranging from colourful budgerigars to chirpy little munnias and even common sparrows that had been dabbed with paint and passed off as some exotic species. Neither Granny nor Grandfather were keen on keeping caged birds as pets, but Aunt Ruby threatened to throw a tantrum if she did not get her way—and Aunt Ruby's tantrums were dreadful to behold.

Anyway, she insisted on keeping the parrot and teaching him to talk. But the bird took an instant dislike to my aunt and resisted all her blandishments.

'Kiss, kiss,' Aunt Ruby would coo, putting her face close to the barge of the cage. But the parrot would back away, his beady little eyes getting even smaller with anger at the prospect of being kissed by Aunt Ruby. And, on one occasion, he lunged forward without warning and knocked my aunt's spectacles off her nose.

After that, Aunt Ruby gave up her endearments and became quite hostile towards the poor bird, making faces at him and calling out, 'Can't talk, can't sing, can't dance!' and other nasty comments.

It fell upon me, then ten years old, to feed the parrot, and he seemed quite happy to receive green chillies and ripe tomatoes from my hands, these delicacies being supplemented by slices of mango, for it was then the mango season. It also gave me an opportunity to consume a couple of mangoes while feeding the parrot.

One afternoon, while everyone was indoors enjoying a siesta, I gave the parrot his lunch and then deliberately left the cage door open. Seconds later, the bird was winging his way to the freedom of the mango orchard.

At the same time Grandfather came on to the veranda, and remarked, 'I see your aunt's parrot has escaped.'

'The door was quite loose,' I said with a shrug. 'Well, I don't suppose we'll see it again.'

Aunt Ruby was upset at first, and threatened to buy another bird. We put her off by promising to buy her a bowl of goldfish.

'But goldfish don't talk,' she protested.

'Well, neither did your bird,' said Grandfather. 'So we'll get you a gramophone. You can listen to Clara Cluck all day. They say she sings like a nightingale.'

I thought we'd never see the parrot again, but he probably missed his green chillies, because a few days later, I found the bird sitting on the veranda railing, looking expectantly at me with his head cocked to one side. Unselfishly, I gave the parrot half of my mango.

While the bird was enjoying the mango, Aunt Ruby emerged from her room and, with a cry of surprise, called out, 'Look, my parrot's come back! He must have missed me!'

With a loud squawk, the parrot flew out of her reach and, perching on the nearest rose bush, glared at Aunt Ruby and shrieked at her in my aunt's familiar tones, 'You're no beauty! Can't talk, can't sing, can't dance!'

Aunt Ruby went ruby red and dashed indoors. But that wasn't the end of the affair. The parrot became a frequent visitor to the garden and veranda and whenever he saw Aunt Ruby he would call out, 'You're no beauty, you're no beauty! Can't sing, can't dance!'

The parrot had learnt to talk after all.

Grandpa Fights an Ostrich

Before my grandfather joined the Indian Railways, he worked for a few years on the East African Railways, and it was during that period that he had his now famous encounter with the ostrich. My childhood was frequently enlivened by this oft-told tale of his, and I give it here in his own words—or as well as I can remember them!

While engaged in the laying of a new railway line, I had a miraculous escape from an awful death. I lived in a small township, but my work lay some twelve miles away, and I had to go to the work site and back on horseback.

One day, my horse had a slight accident, so I decided to do the journey on foot, being a great walker in those days. I also knew of a short cut through the hills that would save me about six miles.

This short cut went through an ostrich farm—or 'camp', as it was called. It was the breeding season. I was fairly familiar with the ways of ostriches, and knew that male birds were very aggressive in the breeding season, ready to attack on the slightest provocation, but I also knew that my dog would scare away any bird that might try to attack me. Strange though it may seem, even the biggest ostrich (and some of them grow to a height of nine feet) will run faster than a racehorse at the sight of even a small dog. So, I felt quite safe in the company of my dog, a mongrel who had adopted me some two months previously.

On arrival at the 'camp', I climbed through the wire fencing and, keeping a good look out, dodged across the open spaces between the thorn bushes. Now and then I caught a glimpse of the birds feeding some distance away.

I had gone about half a mile from the fencing when up started a hare. In an instant my dog gave chase. I tried calling him back, even though I knew it was hopeless. Chasing hares was that dog's passion.

I don't know whether it was the dog's bark or my own shouting, but what I was most anxious to avoid immediately happened. The ostriches were startled and began darting to and fro. Suddenly, I saw a big male bird emerge from a thicket about a hundred yards away. He stood still and stared at me for a few moments. I stared back. Then, expanding his short wings and with his tail erect, he came bounding towards me.

As I had nothing, not even a stick, with which to defend myself, I turned and ran towards the fence. But it was an unequal race. What were my steps of two or three feet against the creature's great strides of sixteen to twenty feet? There was only one hope: to get behind a large bush and try to elude the bird until help came. A dodging game was my only chance.

And so, I rushed for the nearest clump of thorn bushes and waited for my pursuer. The great bird wasted no time—he was immediately upon me.

Then the strangest encounter took place. I dodged this way and that, taking great care not to get directly in front of the ostrich's deadly kick. Ostriches kick forward, and with such terrific force that if you were struck, their huge chisel-like nails would cause you much damage.

I was breathless, and really quite helpless, calling wildly for help as I circled the thorn bush. My strength was ebbing. How much longer could I keep going? I was ready to drop from exhaustion.

As if aware of my condition, the infuriated bird suddenly doubled back on his course and charged straight at me. With a desperate effort I managed to step to one side. I don't know how, but I found myself holding on to one of the creature's wings, quite close to its body.

It was now the ostrich's turn to be frightened. He began to turn, or rather waltz, moving round and round so quickly that my feet were soon swinging out from his body, almost horizontally! All the while the ostrich kept opening and shutting his beak with loud snaps.

Imagine my situation as I clung desperately to the wing of the enraged bird. He was whirling me round and round as though he were a discus-thrower—and I the discus! My arms soon began to ache with the strain, and the swift and continuous circling was making me dizzy. But I knew that if I relaxed my hold, even for a second, a terrible fate awaited me.

Round and round we went in a great circle. It seemed as if that spiteful bird would never tire. And, I knew I could not hold on much longer. Suddenly, the ostrich went into reverse! This unexpected move made me lose my hold and sent me sprawling to the ground. I landed in a heap near the thorn bush and in an instant, before I even had time to realize what had happened, the big bird was upon me. I thought the end had come. Instinctively, I raised my hands to protect my face. But the ostrich did not strike.

I moved my hands from my face and there stood the creature with one foot raised, ready to deliver a deadly kick! I couldn't move. Was the bird going to play cat-and-mouse with me and prolong the agony?

As I watched, frightened and fascinated, the ostrich turned his head sharply to the left. A second later, he jumped back, turned, and made off as fast as he could go. Dazed, I wondered what had happened to make him beat so unexpected a retreat.

I soon found out. To my great joy, I heard the bark of my truant dog, and the next moment he was jumping around me, licking my face and hands. Needless to say, I returned his caresses most affectionately! And I took good care to see that he did not leave my side until we were well clear of that ostrich 'camp'.

The Elephant and the Cassowary Bird

THE BABY elephant wasn't out of place in our home in north India because India is where elephants belong, and in any case, our house was full of pets brought home by Grandfather, who was in the Forest Service. But the cassowary bird was different. No one had ever seen such a bird before—not in India, that is. Grandfather had picked it up on a voyage to Singapore, where he'd been given the bird by a rubber planter who'd got it from a Dutch trader who'd got it from a man in Indonesia.

Anyway, it ended up at our home in Dehra, and seemed to do quite well in the subtropical climate. It looked like a cross between a turkey and an ostrich, but bigger than the former and smaller than the latter—about five feet in height. It was not a beautiful bird, nor even a friendly one, but it had come to stay, and everyone was curious about it, especially the baby elephant.

Right from the start, the baby elephant took a great interest in the cassowary, a bird unlike any found in the Indian jungles. He would circle round the odd creature, and diffidently examine with his trunk the texture of its stumpy wings. Of course he suspected no evil, and his childlike curiosity encouraged him to take liberties which resulted in an unpleasant experience.

Noticing the baby elephant's attempts to make friends with the rather morose cassowary, we felt a bit apprehensive. Self-contained and sullen, the big bird responded only by slowly and slyly raising one of its powerful legs, in the meantime gazing into space with an innocent air. We knew what the gesture meant; we had seen that treacherous leg raised on many an occasion, and suddenly shooting out with a force that would have done credit to a vicious camel. In fact, camel and cassowary kicks are delivered on the same plan, except that the camel kicks backward like a horse and the bird forward.

We wished to spare our baby elephant a painful experience, and led him away from the bird. But he persisted in his friendly overtures, and one morning, he received an ugly reward. Rapid as lightning, the cassowary hit straight from the hip and knee joints, and the elephant ran squealing to Grandfather.

For several days he avoided the cassowary, and we thought he had learnt his lesson. He crossed and recrossed the compound and the garden, swinging his trunk, thinking furiously. Then, a week later, he appeared on the veranda at breakfast time in his usual cheery, childlike fashion, sidling up to the cassowary as if nothing had happened.

We were struck with amazement at this and so, it seemed, was the bird. Had the painful lesson already been forgotten, and by a member of the elephant tribe noted for its ability to never forget? Another dose of the same medicine would serve the booby right.

The cassowary once more began to draw up its fighting leg with sinister determination. It was nearing the true position for the master kick, kung fu style, when all of a sudden the baby elephant seized with his trunk the cassowary's other leg and pulled it down. There was a clumsy flapping of wings, a tremendous swelling of the bird's wattle, and an undignified getting up, as if it were a floored boxer doing his best to beat the count of ten. The bird then marched off with an attempt to look stately and unconcerned, while we at the breakfast table were convulsed with laughter.

After this, the cassowary bird gave the baby elephant as wide a berth as possible. But they were not forced to coexist for very long. The baby elephant, getting bulky and cumbersome, was sold and now lives in a zoo where he is a favourite with young visitors who love to take rides on his back.

As for the cassowary, he continued to grace our veranda for many years, gaped at but not made much of, while entering on a rather friendless old age.

Exciting Encounters

THE FOLLOWING day, Mehmoud was making lamb chops. I liked lamb chops. Mehmoud knew I liked them, and he had an extra chop ready for me, just in case I felt like a pre-lunch snack.

'What was Jim Corbett's favourite dish?' I asked, while dealing with the succulent chop.

'Oh, he liked roast duck. Used to shoot them as they flew up from the jheel.'

'What's a jheel, Mehmoud?'

'A shallow sort of lake. In places you could walk about in the water. Different types of birds would come there in the winter—ducks and geese and all kinds of baglas—herons, you call them. The baglas are not good to eat, but the ducks make a fine roast.

'So we camped beside the jheel and lived on roast duck for a week until everyone was sick of it.'

'Did you go swimming in the jheel?'

'No, it was full of muggers—those long-nosed crocodiles—they'll snap you up if you come within their range! Nasty creatures, those muggermuch. One of them nearly got me.'

'How did that happen, Mehmoud-bhai?'

'Oh, baba, just the memory of it makes me shudder! I'd given everyone their dinner and retired to my tent. It was a hot night and we couldn't sleep. Swarms of mosquitoes rose from the jheel, invaded the tent, and attacked me on the face and arms and feet. I dragged my camp cot outside the tent, hoping the breeze would keep the mosquitoes away. After some time they moved on, and I fell asleep, wrapped up in my bedsheet. Towards dawn, I felt my cot quivering, shaking. Was it an earthquake? But no one else was awake. And then the cot started moving! I sat up, looked about me. The cot was moving steadily forward in the direction of the water. And beneath it, holding us up, was a beastly crocodile!

'It gave me the fright of my life, baba. A muggermuch beneath my bed, and I upon it! I cried out for help. Carpet-sahib woke up, rushed out of his tent, his gun in his hands. But it was still dark, and all he could see was my bed moving rapidly towards the jheel.

'Just before we struck the water, I leapt from the cot, and ran up the bank, calling for help. Carpet-sahib saw me then. He ran down the slope, firing at the moving cot. I don't know if he hit the horrible creature, but there was a big splash, and it disappeared into the jheel.'

'And did you recover the cot?'

'No, it floated away and then sank. We did not go after it.'

'And what did Corbett say afterwards?'

'He said I had shown great presence of mind. He said he'd never seen anyone make such a leap for safety!'

'You were a hero, Mehmoud!'

'Thank you, baba. There's time for another lamb chop, if you're hungry.'

'I'm hungry,' I said. 'There's still an hour left to lunchtime. But tell me more about your time with Jim Corbett. Did he like your cooking?'

'Oh, *he* liked it well enough, but his sister was very fussy.'

'He had his sister with him?'

'That's right. He never married, so his sister looked after the household and the shopping and everything connected to the kitchen—except when we were in camp. Then I had a free hand. Carpet-sahib wasn't too fussy about his food, especially when he was out hunting. A sandwich or paratha would keep him going. But if he had guests, he felt he had to give them the best, and then it was hard work for me.

'For instance, there was the Raja of Janakpur, a big, fat man who was very fond of eating—between meals, during meals and after meals. I don't know why he bothered to come on these shikar trips when he could have stayed at home in his palace and feasted day and night. But he needed trophies to hang on the walls of his palace. You were not considered a great king unless your walls were decorated with the stuffed heads of tigers, lions, antelopes, bears—anything that looked dangerous. The Raja could eat and drink all day, but he couldn't go home without a trophy. So he would be hoisted onto an elephant, and sit there in state, firing away at anything that moved in the jungle. He seldom shot anything, but Carpet-sahib would help him out by bringing down a stag or a leopard, and congratulating the Raja on his skill and accuracy.

'They weren't all like that, but some of the Rajas were stupid or even mad. And the Angrej-sahibs—the English—were no better. They, too, had to prove their manliness by shooting a tiger or a leopard. Carpet-sahib was always in demand, because he lived at the edge of the jungle and knew where to look for different animals.

'The Raja of Janakpur was safe on an elephant, but one day he made the mistake of walking into the jungle on foot.

He hadn't gone far when he met a wild boar running at him. A wild boar may not look very dangerous, but it has deadly tusks and is quick to use them. Before the Raja could raise the gun to his shoulder, the pig charged at him. The Raja dropped his gun, turned and ran for his life. But he couldn't run very fast or very far. He tripped and fell, and the boar was almost upon him when I happened along, looking for twigs to make a fire. Luckily, I had a small axe in my hand. I struck the boar over the head. It turned and rammed one of its tusks into my thigh. I struck at it again and again, till it fell dead at my feet. The Raja was nowhere in sight.

'As soon as he got into camp, he sent for his servants and made a hurried departure. Didn't even thank me for saving his life.'

'Were you hurt badly, Mehmoud?'

'I was out of action for a few days. The wound took time to heal. My new masalchi did all the cooking, and the food was so bad that most of the guests left in a hurry. I still have the scar. See, baba!'

Mehmoud drew up his pyjamas and showed me a deep scar on his right thigh.

'You were a hero, Mehmoud,' I said. 'You deserved a reward.'

'My reward is here, baba, preparing these lamb chops for you. Come on, have another. Your parents won't notice if they run short at lunch.'

Uncle Ken's Rumble in the Jungle

UNCLE KEN drove Grandfather's old Fiat along the forest road at an incredible 30 mph, scattering pheasants, partridges and jungle fowl as he went along. He had come in search of the disappearing red jungle fowl, and I could see why the bird had disappeared. Too many noisy human beings had invaded its habitat.

By the time we reached the forest rest house, one of the car doors had fallen off its hinges, and a large lantana bush had got entwined in the bumper.

'Never mind,' said Uncle Ken. 'It's all part of the adventure.'

The rest house had been reserved for Uncle Ken, thanks to Grandfather's good relations with the forest department. But I was the only other person in the car. No one else would trust himself or herself to Uncle Ken's driving. He treated a car as though it were a low-flying aircraft having some difficulty in getting off the runway.

As we arrived at the rest house, a number of hens made a dash for safety.

'Look, jungle fowl!' exclaimed Uncle Ken.

'Domestic fowl,' I said. 'They must belong to the forest guards.'

I was right, of course. One of the hens was destined to be served up as chicken curry later that day. The jungle birds avoided the neighbourhood of the rest house, just in case they were mistaken for poultry and went into the cooking pot.

Uncle Ken was all for starting his search right away, and after a brief interval during which we were served tea and pakoras (prepared by the forest guard, who, it turned out, was also a good cook), we set off on foot into the jungle in search of the elusive red jungle fowl.

'No tigers around here, are there?' asked Uncle Ken, just to be on the safe side.

'No tigers on this range,' said the guard. 'Just elephants.'

Uncle Ken wasn't afraid of elephants. He'd been on numerous elephants rides at the Lucknow zoo. He'd also seen Sabu in *Elephant Boy*.

A small wooden bridge took us across a little river, and then we were in the jungle, following the forest guard who led us along a path that was frequently blocked by broken tree branches and pieces of bamboo.

'Why all these broken branches?' asked Uncle Ken.

'The elephants, sir,' replied our guard. 'They passed through last night. They like certain leaves, as well as young bamboo shoots.'

We saw a number of spotted deer and several pheasants, but no red jungle fowl.

That evening, we sat out on the veranda of the rest house. All was silent except for the distant trumpeting of elephants. Then, from the stream, came the chanting of hundreds of frogs.

There were tenors and baritones, sopranos and contraltos, and occasionally a bass deep enough to have pleased the great Chaliapin. They sang duets and quartets from *La Bohème* and other Italian operas, drowning out all other jungle sounds except for the occasional cry of a jackal doing his best to join in.

'We might as well sing too,' said Uncle Ken, and began singing 'Indian Love Call' in his best Nelson Eddy manner.

The frogs fell silent, obviously awestruck; but instead of receiving an answering love call, Uncle Ken was answered by even more strident jackal calls—not one, but several—with the result that all self-respecting denizens of the forest fled from the vicinity, and we saw no wildlife that night apart from a frightened rabbit that sped across the clearing and vanished into the darkness.

Early next morning, we renewed our efforts to track down the red jungle fowl, but it remained elusive. Returning to the rest house dusty and weary, Uncle Ken exclaimed: 'There it is—a red jungle fowl.'

But it turned out to be the caretaker's cock bird, a handsome fellow all red and gold, but not the jungle variety.

Disappointed, Uncle Ken decided to return to civilization. Another night in the rest house did not appeal to him. He had run out of songs to sing.

In any case, the weather had changed overnight and a light drizzle was falling as we started out. This had turned to a steady downpour by the time we reached the bridge across the Suseva river. And standing in the middle of the bridge was an elephant.

He was a long tusker and he didn't look too friendly.

Uncle Ken blew his horn, and that was a mistake.

It was a strident, penetrating horn, highly effective on city roads but out of place in the forest.

The elephant took it as a challenge, and returned the blast of the horn with a shrill trumpeting of its own. It took a few steps forward. Uncle Ken put the car into reverse.

'Is there another way out of here?' he asked.

'There's a side road,' I said, recalling an earlier trip with

Grandfather. 'It will take us to the Kansrao railway station.'

'What, ho!' cried Uncle Ken. 'To the station we go!'

And he turned the car and drove back until we came to the turning.

The narrow road was now a rushing torrent of rain water and all Uncle Ken's driving skills were put to the test. He had on one occasion driven through a brick wall, so he knew all about obstacles; but they were usually stationary ones.

'More elephants,' I said, as two large pachyderms loomed out of the rain-drenched forest.

'Elephants to the right of us, elephants to the left of us!' chanted Uncle Ken, misquoting Tennyson's 'Charge of the Light Brigade'. 'Into the valley of death rode the six hundred!'

'There are now three of them,' I observed.

'Not my lucky number,' said Uncle Ken and pressed hard on the accelerator. We lurched forward, almost running over a terrified barking deer.

'Is four your lucky number, Uncle Ken?'

'Why do you ask?'

'Well, there are now four of them behind us. And they are catching up quite fast!'

'I see the station ahead,' cried Uncle Ken, as we drove into a clearing where a tiny railway station stood like a beacon of safety in the wilderness.

The car came to a grinding halt. We abandoned it and ran for the building.

The stationmaster saw our predicament, and beckoned to us to enter the station building, which was little more than a two-room shed and platform. He took us inside his tiny control room and shut the steel gate behind us.

'The elephants won't bother you here,' he said. 'But say goodbye to your car.'

We looked out of the window and were horrified to see Grandfather's Fiat overturned by one of the elephants, while another proceeded to trample it underfoot. The other elephants joined in the mayhem and soon the car was a flattened piece of junk.

'I'm stationmaster Abdul Ranf,' the stationmaster introduced himself. 'I know a good scrap dealer in Doiwala. I'll give you his address.'

'But how do we get out of here?' asked Uncle Ken.

'Well, it's only an hour's walk to Doiwala, but not with those elephants around. Stay and have a cup of tea. The Dehra Express will pass through shortly. It stops for a few minutes. And it's only half-an-hour to Dehra from here.' He punched out a couple of rail tickets. 'Here you are, my friends. Just two rupees each. The cheapest rail journey in India. And these tickets carry an insurance value of two lakh rupees each, should an accident befall you between here and Dehradun.'

Uncle Ken's eyes lit up.

'You mean, if one of us falls out of the train?' he asked.

'Out of the moving train,' clarified the stationmaster. 'There will be an enquiry, of course, some people try to fake an accident.'

But Uncle Ken decided against falling out of the train and making a fortune. He'd had enough excitement for the day. We got home safely enough, taking a pony cart from Dehradun station to our house.

'Where's my car?' asked Grandfather, as we staggered up the veranda steps.

'It had a small accident,' said Uncle Ken. 'We left it outside the Kansrao railway station. I'll collect it later.'

'I'm starving,' I said. 'Haven't eaten since morning.'

'Well, come and have your dinner,' said Granny. 'I've made something special for you. One of your grandfather's hunting friends sent us a jungle fowl. I've made a nice roast. Try it with apple sauce.'

Uncle Ken did not ask if the jungle fowl was red, grey, or technicoloured. He was the first to the dining table.

Granny had anticipated this, and served me with a chicken leg, giving the other leg to Grandfather.

'I rather fancy the breast myself,' she said, and this left Uncle Ken with a long and scrawny neck—which was more than he deserved.

Owls in the Family

ONE MORNING we found a full-fledged baby spotted owlet on the ground by the veranda steps. When Grandfather picked it up, it hissed and clacked its bill, but, after a meal of raw meat and water, settled down for the day under my bed.

The spotted owlet, even when full grown, is only the size of a myna, and has none of the sinister appearance of the larger owls. A pair of them may often be found in an old mango or tamarind tree, and by tapping on the tree trunk you may be able to persuade the bird to show an enquiring face at the entrance to its hole. The bird is not normally afraid of man, nor is it strictly a night-bird; but it prefers to stay at home during the day, as it is sometimes attacked by other birds, who consider all owls as their enemies.

The little owlet was quite happy under my bed. The following day a second owlet was found in almost the same place on the veranda, and only then did we realize that where the rainwater pipe emerged through the roof, there was a rough sort of nest, from which the birds had fallen. We took the second young owl to join the first, and fed them both. When I went to bed they were on the ledge just inside the mosquito netting, and, later in the night, their mother found them there. From outside she crooned and gurgled for a long time, and in the morning I found that she had left a mouse with its tail tucked through the mosquito net! Obviously, she placed no reliance on me as a foster-parent.

The young birds throve and, ten days later at dawn, Grandfather and I took them into the garden to release them. I had placed one on a branch of the mango tree, and was stooping to pick up the other, when I received quite a heavy blow on the back of my head. A second or two later, the mother owl swooped down at Grandfather, but he was agile enough to duck out of its way. Quickly, I placed the second owl under the mango tree. Then, from a safe distance, we watched the mother fly down and lead her offspring into the long grass at the edge of the garden.

We thought she would take her family away from the vicinity of our rather strange household; but next morning, on coming out of my room, I found two young owls standing on the wall just outside the door! I ran to tell Grandfather, and, when we came back, we found the mother sitting on the bird-bath ten yards away. She was evidently feeling sorry for her behaviour the previous day, because she greeted us with a soft 'whoo-whoo'.

'Now there's an unselfish mother for you!' said Grandfather. 'It's obvious she'd like them to have a good home. And they're probably getting a bit too big for her to manage.'

So the two owlets became regular members of our household, and, strangely enough, were among the few pets that Grandmother took a liking to. She objected to all snakes, most monkeys, and some crows, but she took quite a fancy to the owls, and frequently fed them on spaghetti. They seemed quite fond of spaghetti. In fact, the owls became so attached to Grandmother that they began to show affection towards anyone in a petticoat, including Aunt Mabel, who was terrified of them. She would run shrieking from the room every time one of the birds sidled up to her in a friendly manner.

Forgetful of the fact that Grandfather and I had reared them, the owls would sometimes swell their feathers and snap at anyone in trousers. To avoid displeasing them, Grandfather wore a petticoat at feeding time. This mild form of transvestism appeared to satisfy them. I compromised by wearing an apron.

In response to Grandmother's voice, the owlets would make sounds as gentle and soothing as the purring of a cat; but when wild owls were around, ours would rend the night with blood-curdling shrieks. Their nightly occupation was catching beetles, with which the kitchen-quarters were infested at the time. With their sharp eyes and powerful beaks, they were excellent pest destroyers.

The owls loved to sit and splash in a shallow dish, especially if cold water was poured over them from a jug at the same time. They would get thoroughly wet, jump out on to a perch, shake themselves, then return for a second splash and sometimes a third. During the day they dozed in large cages under the trees in the garden. They needed cages for protection against attacks from wild birds. At night they had the freedom of the house, where they exercised their wings as much as they liked. Superstitious folk, who dread the cry of the owl, may be interested to know that—mice excepted—there were no untoward deaths in the house during the owls' residence.

Looking back on those owlish days, I carry in my mind a picture of Grandmother with a contented look in her rocking-chair. Once, on entering her room while she was having an afternoon nap, I saw that one of the owls had crawled up her pillow till its head was snuggled under her ear. Both Grandmother and the little owl were snoring.

Those Three Bears

MOST HIMALAYAN villages lie in the valleys, where there are small streams, some farmland, and protection from the biting winds that come through the mountain passes in winter. The houses are usually made of large stones and have sloping slate roofs so the heavy monsoon rain can run off easily. During the sunny autumn months, the roofs are often covered with pumpkins, left there to ripen in the sun.

One October night, when I was sleeping at a friend's house in a village in these hills, I was awakened by a rumbling and thumping on the roof. I woke my friend and asked him what was happening.

'It's only a bear,' he said.

'Is it trying to get in?'

'No. It's after the pumpkins.'

A little later, when we looked out of a window, we saw a black bear making off through a field, leaving a trail of half-eaten pumpkins.

In winter, when snow covers the higher ranges, the Himalayan bears come to lower altitudes in search of food. Sometimes they forage in fields and because they are shortsighted and suspicious of anything that moves, they can be dangerous. But, like most wild animals, they avoid humans as much as possible.

Village folk always advise me to run downhill if chased by a bear. They say bears find it easier to run uphill than down. I am yet to be chased by a bear, and will happily skip the experience. But I have seen a few of these mountain bears in India, and they are always fascinating to watch.

Himalayan bears enjoy pumpkins, corn, plums, and apricots. Once, while I was sitting in an oak tree hoping to see a pair of pine martens that lived nearby, I heard the whining grumble of a bear, and presently a small bear ambled into the clearing beneath the tree.

He was little more than a cub, and I was not alarmed. I sat very still, waiting to see what he would do.

He put his nose to the ground and sniffed his way along until he came to a large anthill. Here he began huffing and puffing, blowing rapidly in and out of his nostrils, so that the dust from the anthill flew in all directions. But the anthill had been deserted, and so, grumbling, the bear made his way up a nearby plum tree. Soon he was perched high in the branches. It was then that he saw me.

The bear at once scrambled several feet higher up the tree and lay flat on a branch. Since it wasn't a very big branch, there was a lot of bear showing on either side. He tucked his head behind another branch. He could no longer see me, so he apparently was satisfied that he was hidden, although he couldn't help grumbling.

Like all bears, this one was full of curiosity. So, slowly, inch by inch, his black snout appeared over the edge of the branch. As soon as he saw me, he drew his head back and hid his face.

He did this several times. I waited until he wasn't looking, then moved some way down my tree. When the bear looked over and saw that I was missing, he was so pleased that he stretched right across to another branch and helped himself to a plum. I couldn't help bursting into laughter.

The startled young bear tumbled out of the tree, dropped through the branches some fifteen feet, and landed with a thump in a pile of dried leaves. He was unhurt, but fled from the clearing, grunting and squealing all the way.

Another time, my friend Prem told me, a bear had been active in his cornfield. We took up a post at night in an old cattle shed, which gave a clear view of the moonlit field.

A little after midnight, a female bear came down to the edge of the field. She seemed to sense that we had been about. She was hungry, however. So, after standing on her hind legs and peering around to make sure the field was empty, she came cautiously out of the forest.

Her attention was soon distracted by some Tibetan prayer flags, which had been strung between two trees. She gave a grunt of disapproval and began to back away, but the fluttering of the flags was a puzzle that she wanted to solve. So she stopped and watched them.

Soon the bear advanced to within a few feet of the flags, examining them from various angles. Then, seeing that they posed no danger, she went right up to the flags and pulled them down. Grunting with apparent satisfaction, she moved into the field of corn.

Prem had decided that he didn't want to lose any more of his crop, so he started shouting. His children woke up and soon came running from the house, banging on empty kerosene tins.

Deprived of her dinner, the bear made off in a bad temper. She ran downhill at a good speed, and I was glad that I was not in her way.

Uphill or downhill, an angry bear is best given a very wide path.

Visitors from the Forest

Visitors from the Forest

WHEN MIST fills the Himalayan valleys, and heavy monsoon rain sweeps across the hills, it is natural for wild creatures to seek shelter. And sometimes my cottage in the forest is the most convenient refuge.

There is no doubt I make things easier for all concerned by leaving most of my windows open. I like plenty of fresh air indoors, and if a few birds, beasts and insects come in too, they're welcome, provided they don't make too much of a nuisance of themselves.

I must confess, I did lose patience with a bamboo beetle who blundered in the other night and fell into the water jug. I rescued him and pushed him out of the window. A few seconds later he came whirring in again, and with unerring accuracy landed with a plop in the same jug. I fished him out once more and offered him the freedom of the night. But attracted no doubt by the light and warmth of my small sitting room, he came buzzing back, circling the room like a helicopter looking for a place to land. Quickly, I covered the water jug. He landed in a bowl of wild dahlias, and I allowed him to remain there, comfortably curled up in the hollow of a flower.

Sometimes during the day, a bird visits me—a deep blue whistling thrush, hopping about on long, dainty legs, too nervous to sing. She perches on the windowsill, looking out at the rain. She does not permit any familiarity. But if I sit quietly in my chair she will sit quietly on my windowsill, glancing quickly at me now and then to make sure I am keeping my distance. When the rain stops, she glides away, and it is only then, confident in her freedom, that she bursts into full-throated song, her broken but haunting melody echoing down the ravine.

A squirrel comes sometimes, when his home in the oak tree gets waterlogged. Apparently he is a bachelor; anyway, he lives alone. He knows me well, this squirrel, and is bold enough to climb on to the dining table looking for titbits which he always finds because I leave them there deliberately. Had I met him when he was a youngster, he would have learnt to eat from my hand; but I have only been here for a few months. I like it this way. I am not looking for pets; these are simply guests.

Last week, as I was sitting down at my desk to write a long-deferred article, I was startled to see an emerald-green praying mantis sitting on my writing pad. He peered at me with his protuberant glass-bead eyes, and I stared down at him through my glasses. When I gave him a prod, he moved off in a leisurely way. Later, I found him examining the binding of *Leaves of Grass;* perhaps he had found a succulent bookworm. He disappeared for a couple of days, and then I found him on my dressing table, preening himself before the mirror.

Out in the garden, I spotted another mantis, perched on the jasmine bush. Its arms were raised like a boxer's. Perhaps they are a pair, I thought, and went indoors, fetched my mantis and placed him on the jasmine bush opposite his fellow insect. He did not like what he saw—no comparison with his own image!—and made off in a hurry.

My most interesting visitor comes at night, when the lights are still burning—a tiny bat who prefers to fly in through the open door, and will use the window only if there is no alternative. His object is to snap up the moths who cluster round the lamps.

All the bats I have seen fly fairly high, keeping near the ceiling; but this particular bat flies in low like a dive bomber, zooming in and out of chair legs and under tables. Once he passed straight between my legs. Has his radar gone wrong, I wondered, or is he just plain mad?

I went to my shelves of natural history and looked up bats, but could find no explanation for this erratic behaviour. As a last resort, I turned to an ancient volume, Sterndale's *Indian Mammalia* (Calcutta, 1884), and in it, to my delight, found what I was looking for: 'A bat found near Mussoorie by Captain Hutton, on the southern range of hills at 1,800 metres; head and body about three centimetres, skims close to the ground, instead of flying high as bats generally do. Habitat, Jharipani, north-west Himalayas.' Apparently, the bat was rare even in 1884.

Perhaps I have come across one of the few surviving members of the species. Jharipani is only three kilometres from where I live. I am happy that this bat survives in my small corner of the woods, and I undertake to celebrate it in prose and verse. Once, I found it suspended upside down from the railing at the foot of my bed. I decided to leave it there. For a writer alone in the woods, even an eccentric bat is welcome company.

Birdsong in the Hills

Bird-watching is more difficult in the hills than on the plains. Many birds are difficult to spot against the dark green of the trees or the varying shades of the hillsides. Large gardens and open fields make bird-watching much easier on the plains; but up here in the mountains one has to be quick of eye to spot a flycatcher flitting from tree to tree, or a mottled brown treecreeper ascending the trunk of an oak or spruce. But few birds remain silent, and one learns of their presence from their calls or songs. Birdsong is with you wherever you go in the hills, from the foothills to the tree line; and it is often easier to recognize a bird from its voice than from its colourful but brief appearance.

The barbet is one of those birds which are heard more than they are seen. Summer visitors to our hill stations must have heard their monotonous, far-reaching call, *pee-oh, pee-oh,* or *un-nee-ow, un-nee-ow.* They would probably not have seen the birds, as they keep to the tops of high trees where they are not easily distinguished from the foliage. Apart from that, the sound carries for about half a mile, and as the bird has the habit of turning its head from side to side while calling, it is very difficult to know in which direction to look for it.

Barbets love listening to their own voices and often two or three birds answer each other from different trees, each trying to outdo the other in a shrill shouting match. Most birds are noisy during the mating season. Barbets are noisy all the year round!

Some people like the barbet's call and consider it both striking and pleasant. Some don't like it and simply consider it striking!

In parts of the Garhwal Himalayas, there is a legend that the bird is the reincarnation of a moneylender who died of grief at the unjust termination of a law suit. Eternally his plaint rises to heaven, *un-nee-ow, un-nee-ow!* which means, 'injustice, injustice'.

Barbets are found throughout the tropical world, but probably the finest of these birds is the Great Himalayan Barbet. Just over a foot in length, it has a massive yellow bill, almost as large as that of a toucan. The head and neck are a rich violet; the upper back is olive brown with pale green streaks. The wings are green, washed with blue, brown and yellow. In spite of all these brilliant colours, the barbet is not easily distinguished from its leafy surroundings. It goes for the highest tree-tops and seldom comes down to earth.

Hodgson's Grey-Headed Flycatcher-Warbler is the long name that ornithologists, in their infinite wisdom, have given to a very small bird. This tiny bird is heard, if not seen, more often than any other bird throughout the Western Himalayas. It is almost impossible to visit any hill station between Naini Tal and Dalhousie without noticing this warbler; its voice is heard in every second tree; and yet there are few who can say what it looks like.

Its song (if you can call it that) is not very musical, and Douglas Dewar in writing about it was reminded of a notice that once appeared in a third-rate music hall: The audience is respectfully requested not to throw things at the pianist. He is doing his best.

Our little warbler does his best, incessantly emitting four or five unmusical but joyful and penetrating notes.

He is much smaller than a sparrow, being only some four inches in length, of which one-third consists of his tail. His lower plumage is bright yellow, his upper parts olive green; the head and neck are grey, the head being set off by cream-coloured eyebrows. He is an active little bird always on the move, and both he and his mate, and sometimes a few friends, hop about from leaf to leaf, looking for insects both large and small. And the way he puts away an inch-long caterpillar would please the most accomplished spaghetti eater!

Another tiny bird more often heard than it is seen is the Green-Backed Tit, a smart little bird about the size of a sparrow. It constantly utters a sharp, rather metallic but not unpleasant, call which sounds like 'kiss me, kiss me, kiss me...'

Another fine singer is the sunbird, which is found in Kumaon and Garhwal. But perhaps the finest songster is the Grey-Winged Ouzel. Throughout the early summer he makes the wooded hillsides ring with his blackbird-like melody. The hill people call this bird the Kastura or Kasturi, a name also applied to the Himalayan Whistling Thrush. But the whistling thrush has a yellow bill, whereas the ouzel is red-billed and is much the sweeter singer.

Nightjars (or goatsuckers, to give them their ancient name) are birds that lie concealed during the day in shady woods, coming out at dusk on silent wings to hunt for insects. The nightjar has a huge frog-like mouth, but is best recognized by its long tail and wings and its curiously silent flight. After dusk and just before dawn, you can hear its curious call, *tonk-tonk,*

tonk-tonk—a note like that produced by striking a plank with a hammer.

As we pass from the plains to the hills, the traveller is transported from one bird realm to another.

Rajpur is separated from Mussoorie by a five-mile footpath, and within that brief distance we find the caw of the house crow replaced by the deeper note of the corby. Instead of the crescendo shriek of the koel, the double note of the cuckoo meets the ear. For the eternal cooing of the little brown dove, the melodious kokla green pigeon is substituted. The harsh cries of the rose-ringed parakeets give place to the softer call of the slate-headed species. The dissonant voices of the seven sisters no longer issue from the bushes; their place is taken by the weird but more pleasing calls of the Himalayan streaked laughing thrushes.

When I first came to live in the hills, it was the song of the Himalayan whistling thrush that caught my attention. I did not see the bird that day. It kept to the deep shadows of the ravine below the old stone cottage.

The following day I was sitting at my window, gazing out at the new leaves on the walnut and wild pear trees. All was still, the wind was at peace with itself, the mountains brooded massively under the darkening sky. And then, emerging from the depths of that sunless chasm like a dark sweet secret, came the indescribably beautiful call of the whistling thrush.

It is a song that never fails to thrill and enchant me. The bird starts with a hesitant schoolboy whistle, as though trying out the tune; then, confident of the melody, it bursts into full song, a crescendo of sweet notes and variations that ring clearly across the hillside. Suddenly the song breaks off right in the middle of a cadenza, and I am left wondering what happened to make the bird stop so suddenly.

At first the bird was heard but never seen. Then one day I found the whistling thrush perched on the broken garden fence. He was deep glistening purple, his shoulders flecked with white; he had sturdy black legs and a strong yellow beak. A dapper fellow who would have looked just right in a top hat! When he saw me coming down the path, he uttered a sharp *kree-ee*—unexpectedly harsh when compared to his singing—and flew off into the shadowed ravine.

As the months passed, he grew used to my presence and became less shy. Once the rainwater pipes were blocked, and this resulted in an overflow of water and a small permanent puddle under the steps. This became the whistling thrush's favourite bathing place. On sultry summer afternoons, while I was taking a siesta upstairs, I would hear the bird flapping about in the rainwater pool. A little later, refreshed and sunning himself on the roof, he would treat me to a little concert—performed, I could not help feeling, especially for my benefit.

It was Govind, the milkman, who told me the legend of the whistling thrush, locally called Kastura by the hill people, but also going by the name of Krishan-patti.

According to the story, Lord Krishna fell asleep near a mountain stream and while he slept, a small boy made off with the god's famous flute. Upon waking and finding his flute gone, Krishna was so angry that he changed the culprit into a bird. But having once played on the flute, the bird had learnt bits and pieces of Krishna's wonderful music. And so he continued, in his disrespectful way, to play the music of the gods, only stopping now and then (as the whistling thrush does) when he couldn't remember the tune.

It wasn't long before my whistling thrush was joined by a female, who looked exactly like him. (I am sure there are subtle points of difference, but not to my myopic eyes!) Sometimes they gave solo performances, sometimes they sang duets; and these, no doubt, were love calls, because it wasn't long before the pair were making forays into the rocky ledges of the ravine, looking for a suitable maternity home. But a few breeding seasons were to pass before I saw any of their young.

After almost three years in the hills, I came to the conclusion that these were 'birds for all seasons'. They were liveliest in midsummer; but even in the depths of winter, with snow lying on the ground, they would suddenly start singing, as they flitted from pine to oak to naked chestnut.

As I write, there is a strong wind rushing through the trees and bustling about in the chimney, while distant thunder threatens a storm. Undismayed, the whistling thrushes are calling to each other as they roam the wind-threshed forest.

Whistling thrushes usually nest on rocky ledges near water; but my overtures of friendship may have given my visitors other ideas. Recently, I was away from Mussoorie for about a fortnight. When I returned, I was about to open the window when I noticed a large bundle of ferns, lichen, grass, mud and moss balanced outside on the window ledge. Peering through the glass, I was able to recognize this untidy bundle as a nest.

It meant, of course, that I couldn't open the window, as this would have resulted in the nest toppling over the edge. Fortunately the room had another window and I kept this one open to let in sunshine, fresh air, the music of birds, and, always welcome, the call of the postman! The postman's call may not be as musical as birdsong, but this writer never tires of it, for it heralds the arrival of the occasional cheque that makes it possible for him to live close to nature.

And now, this very day, three pink freckled eggs lie in the cup of moss that forms the nursery in this jumble of a nest. The parent birds, both male and female, come and go, bustling about very efficiently, fully prepared for a great day that's coming soon.

The wild cherry trees, which I grew especially for birds, attract a great many small birds, both when it is in flower and when it is in fruit.

When it is covered with pale pink blossoms, the most common visitor is a little yellow-backed sunbird, who emits a squeaky little song as he flits from branch to branch. He extracts the nectar from the blossoms with his tubular tongue, sometimes while hovering on the wing but usually while clinging to the slender twigs.

Just as some vegetarians will occasionally condescend to eat meat, the sunbird (like the barbet) will vary his diet with insects. Small spiders, caterpillars, beetles, bugs and flies (probably in most cases themselves visitors to these flowers), fall prey to these birds. I have also seen a sunbird flying up and catching insects on the wing.

The flycatchers are gorgeous birds, especially the Paradise Flycatcher with its long white tail and ghost-like flight; and although they are largely insectivorous, like some meat-eaters they will also take a little fruit! And so they will occasionally visit the cherry tree when its sour little cherries are ripening. While travelling over the boughs, they utter twittering notes with occasional louder calls, and now and then the male bird breaks out into a sweet little song, thus justifying the name of Shah Bulbul by which he is known in northern India.

Copperfield in the Jungle

GRANDFATHER NEVER hunted wild animals; he could not understand the pleasure some people obtained from killing the creatures of our forests. Birds and animals, he felt, had as much right to live as humans. There was some justification in killing for food—most animals did—but none at all in killing just for the fun of it.

At the age of twelve, I did not have the same high principles as Grandfather. Nevertheless, I disliked anything to do with shikar or hunting. I found it terribly boring.

Uncle Henry and some of his sporting friends once took me on a shikar expedition into the Terai forests of the Siwaliks. The prospect of a whole week in the jungle as camp follower to several adults with guns filled me with dismay. I knew that long, weary hours would be spent tramping behind these tall, professional-looking huntsmen. They could only speak in terms of bagging this tiger or that wild elephant, when all they ever got, if they were lucky, was a wild hare or a partridge. Tigers and excitement, it seemed, came only to Jim Corbett.

This particular expedition proved to be different from others. There were four men with guns, and at the end of the week, all that they had shot were two miserable, underweight wild fowls. But I managed, on our second day in the jungle, to be left behind at the rest house. And, in the course of a morning's exploration of the old bungalow, I discovered a shelf of books half-hidden in a corner of the back veranda.

Who had left them there? A literary forest officer? A memsahib who had been bored by her husband's camp-fire boasting? Or someone who had no interest in the 'manly' sport of slaughtering wild animals and had brought his library along to pass the time?

Or possibly the poor fellow had gone into the jungle one day, as a gesture towards his more bloodthirsty companions, and been trampled by an elephant, or gored by a wild boar, or (more likely) accidentally shot by one of the shikaris and his sorrowing friends had taken his remains away and left his books behind.

Anyway, there they were—a shelf of some thirty volumes, obviously untouched for many years. I wiped the thick dust off the covers and examined the titles. As my reading tastes had not yet formed, I was willing to try anything. The bookshelf was varied in its contents—and my own interests have since remained fairly universal.

On that fateful day in the forest rest house, I discovered P.G. Wodehouse and read his *Love among the Chickens,* an early Ukridge story and still one of my favourites. By the time the perspiring hunters came home late in the evening, with their spent cartridges and lame excuses, I had made a start with M.R. James's *Ghost Stories of an Antiquary,* which had me hooked on ghost stories for the rest of my life. It kept me awake most of the night, until the oil in the kerosene lamp had finished.

Next morning, fresh and optimistic again, the shikaris set out for a different area, where they hoped to 'bag a tiger'. They had employed a party of villagers to beat the jungle, and all day I could hear their drums throbbing in the distance. This did not prevent me from finishing M.R. James or discovering a book called *A Naturalist on the Prowl* by Edward Hamilton Aitken.

My concentration was disturbed only once, when I looked up and saw a spotted deer crossing the open clearing in front of the bungalow. The deer disappeared among the sal trees, and I returned to my book.

Dusk had fallen when I heard the party returning from the hunt. The great men were talking loudly and seemed excited. Perhaps they had got their tiger. I put down my book and came out to meet them.

'Did you shoot the tiger?' I asked excitedly.

'No, my boy,' said Uncle Henry. 'I think we'll bag it tomorrow. But you should have been with us—we saw a spotted deer!'

There were three days left and I knew I would never get through the entire bookshelf. So I chose *David Copperfield*—my first encounter with Dickens—and settled down on the veranda armchair to make the acquaintance of Mr Micawber and his family, Aunt Betsy Trotwood, Mr Dick, Peggotty, and a host of other larger-than-life people. I think it would be true to say that *David Copperfield* set me off on the road to literature; I identified with young David and wanted to grow up to be a writer like him.

But on my second day with the book an event occurred which disturbed my reading for a little while.

I had noticed, on the previous day, that a number of stray dogs—belonging to watchmen, villagers and forest guards—always hung about the house, waiting for scraps of food to be thrown away. It was ten o'clock in the morning, a time when wild animals seldom come into the open, when I heard a sudden yelp in the clearing. Looking up, I saw a large leopard making off into the jungle with one of the dogs held in its jaws. The leopard had either been driven towards the house by the beaters, or had watched the party leave the bungalow and decided to help itself to a meal.

There was no one else about at the time. Since the dog was obviously dead within seconds of being seized, and the leopard had disappeared, I saw no point in raising an alarm which would have interrupted my reading. So I returned to *David Copperfield*.

It was getting late when the shikaris returned. They were dirty, sweaty, and as usual, disappointed. Next day we were to return to the city, and none of the hunters had anything to show for a week in the jungle. Swear words punctuated their conversation.

'No game left in these… jungles,' said the leading member of the party, famed for once having shot two man-eating tigers and a basking crocodile in rapid succession.

'It's this beastly weather,' said Uncle Henry. 'No rain for months.'

'I saw a leopard this morning,' I said modestly.

But no one took me seriously. 'Did you really?' said the leading hunter, glancing at the book beside me. 'Young Master Copperfield says he saw a leopard!'

'Too imaginative for his age,' said Uncle Henry. 'Comes from reading too much, I suppose.'

'If you were to get out of the house and into the jungle,' said the third member, 'you might really see a leopard! Don't know what young chaps are coming to these days.'

I went to bed early and left them to their tales of the 'good old days' when rhinos, cheetahs, and possibly even the legendary phoenix were still available for slaughter.

Next day the camp broke up and we went our different ways. I was still only half-way through *David Copperfield,* but I saw no reason why it should be left behind to gather dust for another thirty years, and so I took it home with me. I have it still, a reminder of how I failed as a shikari but launched myself on a literary career.

The Hare in the Moon

A LONG TIME ago, when animals could talk, there lived in a forest four wise creatures—a hare, a jackal, an otter and a monkey.

They were good friends, and every evening they would sit together in a forest glade to discuss the events of the day, exchange advice, and make good resolutions. The hare was the noblest and wisest of the four. He believed in the superiority of men and women, and was always telling his friends tales of human goodness and wisdom.

One evening, when the moon rose in the sky—and in those days the moon's face was clear and unmarked—the hare looked up at it carefully and said: 'Tomorrow good men will observe a fast, for I can see that it will be the middle of the month. They will eat no food before sunset, and during the day they will give alms to any beggar or holy man who may meet them. Let us promise to do the same. In that way, we can come a little closer to human beings in dignity and wisdom.'

The others agreed, and then went their different ways.

Next day, the otter got up, stretched himself, and was preparing to get his breakfast when he remembered the vow he had taken with his friends.

'If I keep my word, how hungry I shall be by evening!' he thought. 'I'd better make sure that there's plenty to eat once the fast is over.' He set off towards the river.

A fisherman had caught several large fish early that morning, and had buried them in the sand, planning to return for them later. The otter soon smelt them out.

'A supper all ready for me!' he said to himself. 'But since it's a holy day, I mustn't steal.' Instead he called out: 'Does anyone own this fish?'

There being no answer, the otter carried the fish off to his home, setting it aside for his evening meal. Then he locked his front door and slept all through the day, undisturbed by beggars or holy men asking for alms.

Both the monkey and the jackal felt much the same way when they got up that morning. They remembered their vows but thought it best to have something put by for the evening. The jackal found some stale meat in someone's back yard. 'Ah, that should improve with age,' he thought, and took it home for his evening meal. And the monkey climbed a mango tree and picked a bunch of mangoes. Like the otter, they decided to sleep through the day.

The hare woke early. Shaking his long ears, he came out of his burrow and sniffed the dew-drenched grass.

'When evening comes, I can have my fill of grass,' he thought. 'But if a beggar or holy man comes my way, what can I give him? I cannot offer him grass, and I have nothing else to give. I shall have to offer myself. Most men seem to relish the flesh of the hare. We're good to eat, I'm told.' And pleased with this solution to the problem, he scampered off.

Now God Sakka had been resting on a cloud not far away, and he had heard the hare speaking aloud.

'I will test him,' said the god. 'Surely no hare can be so noble and unselfish.'

Towards evening, God Sakka descended from his cloud, and assuming the form of an old priest, he sat down near the hare's burrow. When the animal came home from his romp, he said: 'Good evening, little hare. Can you give me something to eat? I have been fasting all day, and am so hungry that I cannot pray.'

The hare, remembering his vow, said: 'Is it true that men enjoy eating the flesh of the hare?'

'Quite true,' said the priest.

'In that case,' said the hare, 'since I have no other food to offer you, you can make a meal of me.'

'But I am a holy man, and this is a holy day, and I may not kill any living creature with my own hands.'

'Then collect some dry sticks and set them alight. I will leap into the flames myself, and when I am roasted you can eat me.'

God Sakka marvelled at these words, but he was still not quite convinced, so he caused a fire to spring up from the earth. The hare, without any hesitation, jumped into the flames.

'What's happening?' called the hare after a while. 'The fire surrounds me, but not a hair of my coat is singed. In fact, I'm feeling quite cold!'

As the hare spoke, the fire died down, and he found himself sitting on the cool sweet grass. Instead of the old priest, there stood before him God Sakka in all his radiance.

'I am God Sakka, little hare, and having heard your vow, I wanted to test your sincerity. Such unselfishness of yours deserves immortality. It must be known throughout the world.'

God Sakka then stretched out his hand towards the mountain, and drew from it some of the essence which ran in its veins. This he threw towards the moon, which had just risen, and instantly the outline of the hare appeared on the moon's surface.

Then leaving the hare in a bed of sweet grass, he said: 'For ever and ever, little hare, you shall look down from the moon upon the world, to remind men of the old truth, "Give to others, and the gods will give to you."'

The White Elephant

LONG AGO, when animals could talk like humans, a great herd of elephants lived in a forest near the Himalaya mountains. The finest elephant in the tribe was a rare white animal.

Unfortunately the mother of this elephant was old and blind and although her son gathered sweet wild fruits for her every day, he was often angry to find the other elephants had stolen his mother's food.

'Mother,' he said, 'it would be better if you and I were to go and live alone in a distant cave I have discovered.'

The mother elephant agreed and for a time the two of them lived happily in a peaceful spot near a glade of wild fruit trees. Until one evening they heard loud cries coming from the great forest.

'That is the voice of a man in distress,' said the white elephant. 'I must go and see if I can help him.'

'Do not go, my son,' said his mother. 'I am old and blind but I know the ways of human beings towards us. Your goodness will be rewarded by treachery.'

But the white elephant could not bear to think of anyone in trouble and he hurried down to the lake in the direction of the cries, where he discovered a man who was a forester.

'Don't fear me, stranger,' he said. 'Tell me how I can help you.'

The forester told the white elephant he had been lost for seven days and nights and could not find his way back to Benares where he lived.

'Climb on my back,' said the elephant cheerfully, 'and I will carry you home.'

The elephant carried the man swiftly through the forest until they reached open country; then he left him on the outskirts of the city before returning to his cave.

Now the forester was a greedy and cunning man and he knew that before he left Benares, the king's favourite elephant had died. 'The king would reward me richly,' thought the man, 'if I captured this fine animal for him,' and straightaway he asked for a royal audience.

The king was delighted with the description of the white elephant. 'I would love to possess such a fine creature. Go back to the forest with a band of my most skilful trainers and if they succeed in capturing this rare elephant, you shall be well rewarded.'

The forester had cunningly noted landmarks while riding back to Benares and he led the trainers to the lake where the white elephant was gathering bamboo stems for his mother's evening meal. When the elephant saw the forester with the band of trainers, he knew he had been betrayed.

He tried to escape but the trainers pursued him and soon succeeded in capturing him. Then they led him through the forest and entered Benares in triumph.

The poor mother elephant, waiting for her son to return, felt certain that he had been captured.

'What shall I do without him?' she cried. 'Who will bring

me food and lead me to the lotus lake for water.'

The heart of her son was equally heavy. 'What will she do without me,' he thought, 'if only I had listened to her advice.'

In spite of his unhappy look, the elephant found favour with the king, who declared he would ride no other animal. The elephant's stable was richly decorated in his honour and the king rode him in state through the city.

But a few days later the trainers came to the king in great distress saying, 'Your Majesty, the white elephant is very sick and will eat nothing.'

The king hurried to the stable and when he saw the elephant's look of despair, he said, 'Good animal, how you have changed! Why do you refuse to eat? Anything you wish will be granted to you.'

'Great King,' answered the elephant mournfully, 'all I desire is to return to my poor blind mother in the forest, for while she is alone and starving, how can I eat?'

Now the king was a good king and although he badly wanted the elephant for himself, he said at once, 'Noble animal, your goodness puts mankind to shame. I give you your freedom to return to your mother at once.'

The elephant thanked the king with a loud trumpeting, and left the city and went crashing back through the forest. When he reached the cave, he found to his joy that his mother was still alive.

'Ah, my son,' she said when he told her his story. 'You should have listened to me. Human beings have always brought harm to our race.'

'Not all of them, mother,' he said triumphantly. 'The king is noble and generous or I should still be in captivity. Let's forget the treachery of the forester and think only of the king's goodness!'

The Boy Who Could See Footsteps

About fifty miles from the city of Benares, in India, there once lived, in a great dark cave, a creature called a Yakka. She had the face of a horse and the body of a woman. She was strong and fierce as a tigress. And she lived upon the flesh of any man or beast whom she could trap.

One day the Yakka caught a school teacher who was travelling alone towards Benares. She carried him off with great swiftness into her cave. When she saw that he was young and handsome, she asked him whether, if she spared his life, he would marry her. And the teacher, thinking that of two evils this would be the lesser, agreed to become her husband.

Afterwards the Yakka grew more and more humane and gentle, gave up eating people and tried in various ways to improve her mind. However, she always feared that her teacher-husband would run away if he could, so she used to roll a huge stone in front of the entrance to the cave whenever she went out to collect food. And in this way the poor teacher was kept a prisoner.

The Yakka was happy enough, and spent her days lying in wait for passing caravans. Fearful travellers were only too ready to part with food and spices, and upon these the Yakka and her husband lived. At length a little son was born to them. In spite of being cooped up in a dark, cold cave, he grew into a strong and clever boy. The Yakka was devoted to him and did all she could to make him and his father comfortable and happy. But the poor teacher pined for freedom. He longed for sunshine and fresh breezes, for the sights and sounds of the city.

One day his son said to him, 'Father, why is my mother's face so different from ours?'

'Because she is a Yakka, son, and we are men.'

'Then why do we live with her in this gloomy cave, instead of among our fellows?'

'Because of the great stone which the Yakka rolls in front of the cave's entrance. It is too heavy for me to move. But you have your mother's strength—see if you can move it.'

The boy sprang up and, setting his shoulder to the stone, easily rolled it aside. He seized his father by the hand and they ran until the teacher, unused to the light and air, became half-blind and dizzy from the exertion. Even the boy was breathless. They sat down to rest; but, before they had recovered enough to go on, they heard the thud of the Yakka's feet in pursuit, and she soon caught up with them.

'Oh, thankless husband and more thankless child!' she cried. 'Why do you run away? What did you lack in my home? You lay upon beds of leaf and moss. You ate dates and drank the wine of pomegranates.'

'But, Mother,' answered the boy, 'we lack air and light, and these are more necessary to us than wine and dates.'

'Come back with me and you shall have both,' she said. So they returned, and she broke the great stone into splinters, and allowed them to wander into the woods and up and down the road; but whenever they got more than a kilometre away from the cave they would always hear her great feet thudding after them.

One day the boy found out that his mother's power extended only as far as the river one way, and as far as the mountains the other way. So when she was fast asleep, on a dark night, he and his father crept out of the cave and fled towards the river. They had just managed to reach the bank when they heard the sound of the Yakka's feet thudding after them. But the boy did not pause. He hoisted his father on his back and waded up to his waist in the stream. Then, safe from the Yakka's power, he looked back. 'Come back, come back!' she cried.

'I will return one day,' replied the boy. 'We are men, and it is right that we should dwell among men. But you are my mother and have given me your love. I will return.'

The Yakka knelt upon the river bank and wept tears into the running water; but father and son had already made their way to the other bank. She no longer pleaded with them; but, because she loved her child dearly, she told him he should take from her a talisman that should prove of great value to him in the world of men.

'Take this stone,' she said, throwing it across to him, 'and hang it about your neck. By its power you will be able to see footsteps even twelve years after they have been made upon the ground by the feet of men.'

The boy caught the stone and fastened it round his neck. Then, waving goodbye, he and his father took the road to Benares. All the way the boy saw thousands of footprints—prints that had long since disappeared from the sight of ordinary humans—and at first he was confused by these tell-tale signs of the men and women who had come and gone that way over the years; but he soon got used to them, and even began to single out the more interesting footprints, and by the time they reached Benares, he had come to the conclusion that no two footprints were the same.

As soon as they arrived in the city, they went straight to the king's palace, where the boy's father was appointed a teacher in a school for young princes. The king soon heard from his ministers that the teacher's son had the power of seeing long-vanished footsteps.

'Should any robber tamper with the king's treasury, my son can trace the thief and find the valuables,' the teacher announced to the chief minister. 'Why not ask your royal master to take the boy into his service?'

The king was only too glad to do so, for he was extremely rich and miserly, and lived in daily and nightly fear of being robbed.

'How much does this boy expect us to pay him?' was his first question.

'A thousand rupees daily,' said the minister.

'Too much, too much!' complained the king. But the boy held out for that sum, and the king at last agreed to it.

Some months passed and, as the fame of the boy's gift passed through Benares, no attempts were made to rob the treasury.

The king was still unhappy about the fee he was paying the boy. 'How are we to know that he is not an impostor?' he complained. 'We are paying him a thousand rupees daily, and he does nothing but sit upon an expensive rug near my marble fountain, playing chess with his father and drinking lemonade! I'm being cheated!'

The next night two thieves broke into the vaults where the treasure was kept. They took many jewels and much money, which they placed in sacks. Then they walked three times round the palace, passed through the gardens, climbed the wall by means of a ladder and finally reached a tank in the middle of a meadow. They dropped the sacks into the tank and then disappeared into the night.

Next day, the king raised a terrible outcry. Some of the most precious of the crown jewels had been stolen! The thief must be found! Where was the boy who could see footsteps?

'Here I am, sire,' said the boy, hurrying to the king's audience chamber. 'I shall trace the thieves at once!'

And starting from the vaults, he walked three times round the palace, passed through the gardens, climbed the wall at a certain spot and finally reached the tank in the meadow. He ordered a diver to enter the water and bring up whatever he could find at the bottom.

'I have seen the footsteps of two men all the way,' he said, 'and they are men of distinction.'

For some moments there was deep silence as they all stood around gazing down into the tank.

People clapped and cheered as the diver brought up, one by one, the bags full of treasure. But the king, who appeared disappointed to see how well the boy was earning his salary, whispered to his minister, 'This is all very well. He has recovered the treasure. But can he trace the thieves? Let us test him further.' And turning to the boy, he said aloud, 'Now find me these thieves.'

'That should not be necessary now that the jewels and money are recovered,' said the boy thoughtfully.

But the king insisted. 'I shall cut your salary by half if you cannot find the thieves. My heart longs to punish those rascals.'

'Be careful of what you say, sire,' said the boy. 'If it is someone upon whom the people depend, what shall the people do?'

'Punish him, of course!' said the king, laughing.

'Shall I name the thieves, then?' asked the boy for the last time.

'Yes, or I cut your thousand rupees daily down to a hundred!'

'Yourself and your minister, O King! You are the thieves!'

And when the people learned that their rulers stooped to all this trickery to fill their private coffers with wealth that should have been used for the benefit of the kingdom, they decided that these two were not worthy to hold positions of trust over them. So they dethroned the king and exiled him and his minister, and gave the crown to the boy who saw their footsteps.

And did the boy ever see his mother, the Yakka, again?

No one knew for certain, but it was said that he would mysteriously disappear on full-moon nights. And although his ministers followed him to try and find out where he went, they never succeeded, because the boy was careful not to leave any footprints of his own.

The Tiger King's Gift

LONG AGO, in the days of the ancient Pandya kings of south India, a father and his two sons lived in a village near Madura. The father was an astrologer, but he had never become famous, and so was very poor. The elder son was called Chellan; the younger Gangan. When the time came for the father to put off his earthly body, he gave his few fields to Chellan, and a palm leaf with some words scratched on it to Gangan.

These were the words that Gangan read:

'From birth, poverty;
For ten years, captivity;
On the seashore, death.
For a little while happiness shall follow.'

'This must be my fortune,' said Gangan to himself, 'and it doesn't seem to be much of a fortune. I must have done something terrible in a former birth. But I will go as a pilgrim to Papanasam and do penance. If I can expiate my sin, I may have better luck.'

His only possession was a water jar of hammered copper, which had belonged to his grandfather. He coiled a rope round the jar, in case he needed to draw water from a well. Then he put a little rice into a bundle, said farewell to his brother, and set out.

As he journeyed, he had to pass through a great forest. Soon he had eaten all his food and drunk all the water in his jar. In the heat of the day he became very thirsty.

At last he came to an old, disused well. As he looked down into it, he could see that a winding stairway had once gone round it down to the water's edge, and that there had been four landing places at different heights down this stairway, so that those who wanted to fetch water might descend the stairway to the level of the water and fill their water pots with ease, regardless of whether the well was full, or three-quarters full, or half full or only one-quarter full.

Now the well was nearly empty. The stairway had fallen away. Gangan could not go down to fill his water jar so he uncoiled his rope, tied his jar to it and slowly let it down. To his amazement, as it was going down past the first landing place, a huge striped paw shot out and caught it, and a growling voice called out: 'Oh Lord of Charity, have mercy! The stair is fallen. I die unless you save me! Fear me not. Though King of Tigers, I will not harm you.'

Gangan was terrified at hearing a tiger speak, but his kindness overcame his fear, and with a great effort, he pulled the beast up.

The Tiger King—for it was indeed the Lord of All Tigers—bowed his head before Gangan, and reverently paced around him thrice from right to left as worshippers do round a shrine.

'Three days ago,' said the Tiger King, 'a goldsmith passed by, and I followed him. In terror he jumped down this well and fell on the fourth landing place below. He is there still. When I leaped after him I fell on the first landing place. On the third landing is a rat who jumped in when a great snake chased him.

And on the second landing, above the rat, is the snake who followed him. They will all clamour for you to draw them up.

'Free the snake, by all means. He will be grateful and will not harm you. Free the rat, if you will. But do not free the goldsmith, for he cannot be trusted. Should you free him, you will surely repent of your kindness. He will do you an injury for his own profit. But remember that I will help you whenever you need me.'

Then the Tiger King bounded away into the forest.

Gangan had forgotten his thirst while he stood before the Tiger King. Now he felt it more than before, and again let down his water jar.

As it passed the second landing place on the ruined staircase, a huge snake darted out and twisted itself round the rope. 'Oh, Incarnation of Mercy, save me!' it hissed. 'Unless you help me, I must die here, for I cannot climb the sides of the well. Help me, and I will always serve you!'

Gangan's heart was again touched, and he drew up the snake. It glided round him as if he were a holy being. 'I am the Serpent King,' it said. 'I was chasing a rat. It jumped into the well and fell on the third landing below. I followed, but fell on the second landing. Then the goldsmith leaped in and fell on the fourth landing place, while the tiger fell on the top landing. You saved the Tiger King. You have saved me. You may save the rat, if you wish. But do not free the goldsmith. He is not to be trusted. He will harm you if you help him. But I will not forget you, and will come to your aid if you call upon me.'

Then the King of Snakes disappeared into the long grass of the forest.

Gangan let down his jar once more, eager to quench his thirst. But as the jar passed the third landing, the rat leaped into it.

'After the Tiger King, what is a rat?' said Gangan to himself, and pulled the jar up.

Like the tiger and the snake, the rat did reverence, and offered his services if ever they were needed. And like the tiger and the snake, he warned Gangan against the goldsmith. Then the Rat King—for he was none other—ran off into a hole among the roots of a banyan tree.

By this time, Gangan's thirst was becoming unbearable. He almost flung the water jar down the well. But again the rope was seized, and Gangan heard the goldsmith beg piteously to be hauled up.

'Unless I pull him out of the well, I shall never get any water,' groaned Gangan. 'And after all, why not help the unfortunate man?' So with a great struggle—for he was a very fat goldsmith—Gangan got him out of the well and on to the grass beside him.

The goldsmith had much to say. But before listening to him, Gangan let his jar down into the well a fifth time. And then he drank till he was satisfied.

'Friend and deliverer!' cried the goldsmith. 'Don't believe what those beasts have said about me! I live in the holy city of Tenkasi, only a day's journey north of Papanasam. Come and visit me whenever you are there. I will show you that I am not an ungrateful man.' And he took leave of Gangan and went his way.

'From birth, poverty.'

Gangan resumed his pilgrimage, begging his way to Papanasam. There he stayed many weeks, performing all the ceremonies which pilgrims should perform, bathing at the waterfall, and watching the Brahmin priests feeding the fishes in the sacred stream. He visited other shrines, going as far as Cape Comorin, the southernmost tip of India, where he bathed in the sea. Then he came back through the jungles of Travancore.

He had started on his pilgrimage with his copper water jar and nothing more. After months of wanderings, it was still the only thing he owned. The first prophecy on the palm leaf had already come true: '*From birth, poverty.*'

During his wanderings Gangan had never once thought of the Tiger King and the others, but as he walked wearily along in his rags, he saw a ruined well by the roadside, and it reminded him of his wonderful adventure. And just to see if the Tiger King was genuine, he called out: 'Oh King of Tigers, let me see you!'

No sooner had he spoken than the Tiger King leaped out of the bushes, carrying in his mouth a glittering golden helmet, embedded with precious stones.

It was the helmet of King Pandya, the monarch of the land.

The king had been waylaid and killed by robbers, for the sake of the jewelled helmet; but they in turn had fallen prey to the tiger, who had walked away with the helmet.

Gangan, of course, knew nothing about all this, and when the Tiger King laid the helmet at his feet, he stood stupefied at its splendour and his own good luck.

After the Tiger King had left him, Gangan thought of the goldsmith. 'He will take the jewels out of the helmet, and I will sell some of them. Others I will take home.' So he wrapped the helmet in a rag and made his way to Tenkasi.

In the Tenkasi bazaar he soon found the goldsmith's shop. When they had talked a while, Gangan uncovered the golden helmet. The goldsmith—who knew its worth far better than Gangan—gloated over it, and at once agreed to take out the jewels and sell a few so that Gangan might have some money to spend.

'Now let me examine this helmet at leisure,' said the goldsmith. 'You go to the shrines, worship, and come back. I will then tell you what your treasure is worth.'

Gangan went off to worship at the famous shrines of Tenkasi. And as soon as he had gone, the goldsmith went off to the local magistrate.

'Did not the herald of King Pandya's son come here only yesterday and announce that he would give half his kingdom to anyone who discovered his father's murderer?' he asked. 'Well, I have found the killer. He has brought the king's jewelled helmet to me this very day.'

The magistrate called his guards, and they all hurried to the goldsmith's shop and reached it just as Gangan returned from his tour of the temples.

'Here is the helmet!' exclaimed the goldsmith to the magistrate. 'And here is the villain who murdered the king to get it!'

The guards seized poor Gangan and marched him off to Madura, the capital of the Pandya kingdom, and brought him before the murdered king's son. When Gangan tried to explain about the Tiger King, the goldsmith called him a liar, and the new king had him thrown into the death cell, a deep, well-like pit, dug into the ground in a courtyard of the palace. The only entrance to it was a hole in the pavement of the courtyard. Here Gangan was left to die of hunger and thirst.

At first Gangan lay helpless where he had fallen. Then, looking around him, he found himself on a heap of bones, the bones of those who before him had died in the dungeon; and he was watched by an army of rats who were waiting to gnaw his dead body. He remembered how the Tiger King had warned him against the goldsmith, and had promised help if ever it was needed.

'I need help now,' groaned Gangan, and shouted for the Tiger King, the Snake King, and the Rat King.

For some time nothing happened. Then all the rats in the dungeon suddenly left him and began burrowing in a corner between some of the stones in the wall. Presently, Gangan saw that the hole was quite large, and that many other rats were coming and going, working at the same tunnel. And then the Rat King himself came through the little passage, and he was followed by the Snake King, while a great roar from outside told Gangan that the Tiger King was there.

'We cannot get you out of this place,' said the Snake King. 'The walls are too strong. But the armies of the Rat King will bring rice cakes from the palace kitchens, and sweets from the shops in the bazaars, and rags soaked in water. They will not let you die. And from this day on the tigers and the snakes will slay tenfold, and the rats will destroy grain and cloth as never before. Before long the people will begin to complain. Then, when you hear anyone passing in front of your cell, shout: "These disasters are the results of your ruler's injustice! But I can save you from them!" At first they will pay no attention. But after some time they will take you out, and at your word we will stop the sacking and the slaughter. And then they will honour you.'

'For ten years, captivity.'

For ten years the tigers killed. The serpents struck. The rats destroyed. And at last the people wailed, 'The gods are plaguing us.'

All the while, Gangan cried out to those who came near his cell, declaring that he could save them; they thought he was a madman. So ten years passed, and the second prophecy on the palm leaf was fulfilled.

At last, the Snake King made his way into the palace and

bit the king's only daughter. She was dead in a few minutes.

The king called for all the snake charmers and offered half his kingdom to any one of them who would restore his daughter to life. None of them was able to do so. Then the king's servants remembered the cries of Gangan and remarked that there was a madman in the dungeons who kept insisting that he could bring an end to all their troubles. The king at once ordered the dungeon to be opened. Ladders were let down. Men descended and found Gangan, looking more like a ghost than a man. His hair had grown so long that none could see his face. The king did not remember him, but Gangan soon reminded the king of how he had condemned him without enquiry, on the word of the goldsmith.

The king grovelled in the dust before Gangan, begged forgiveness, and entreated him to restore the dead princess to life.

'Bring me the body of the princess,' said Gangan.

Then he called on the Tiger King and the Snake King to come and give life to the princess. As soon as they entered the royal chamber, the princess was restored to life.

Glad as they were to see the princess alive, the king and his courtiers were filled with fear at the sight of the Tiger King and the Snake King. But the tiger and the snake hurt no one, and at a second prayer from Gangan, they brought life to all those they had slain.

And when Gangan made a third petition, the Tiger, the Snake and the Rat Kings ordered their subjects to stop pillaging the Pandya kingdom, so long as the king did no further injustice.

'Let us find that treacherous goldsmith and put him in the dungeon,' said the Tiger King.

But Gangan wanted no vengeance. That very day he set out for his village to see his brother, Chellan, once more. But when he left the Pandya king's capital, he took the wrong road. After much wandering, he found himself on the seashore.

Now it happened that his brother was also making a journey in those parts, and it was their fate that they should meet by the sea. When Gangan saw his brother, his gladness was so sudden and so great that he fell down dead.

And so the third prophecy was fulfilled:

'On the seashore, death.'

Chellan, as he came along the shore road, had seen a half-ruined shrine of Pillaiyar, the elephant-headed god of good luck. Chellan was a very devout servant of Pillaiyar, and, the day being a festival day, he felt it was his duty to worship the god. But it was also his duty to perform the funeral rites for his brother.

The seashore was lonely. There was no one to help him. It would take hours to collect fuel and driftwood enough for a funeral pyre. For a while Chellan did not know what to do. But at last he took up the body and carried it to Pillaiyar's temple.

Then he addressed the god. 'This is my brother's body,' he said. 'I am unclean because I have touched it. I must go and bathe in the sea. Then I will come and worship you, and afterwards I will burn my brother's body. Meanwhile, I leave it in your care.'

Chellan left, and the god told his attendant *gana*s (goblins) to watch over the body. These *gana*s are inclined to be mischievous, and when the god wasn't looking, they gobbled up the body of Gangan.

When Chellan came back from bathing, he reverently worshipped Pillaiyar. He then looked for his brother's body. It was not to be found. Anxiously he demanded it of the god. Pillaiyar called on his goblins to produce it. Terrified, they confessed to what they had done.

Chellan reproached the god for the misdeeds of his

attendants. And Pillaiyar felt so much pity for him that by his divine power he restored dead Gangan's body to Chellan, and brought Gangan to life again.

The two brothers then returned to King Pandya's capital, where Gangan married the princess and became king when her father died.

And so the fourth prophecy was fulfilled:

'For a little while happiness shall follow.'

But there are wise men who say that the lines of the prophecy were wrongly read and understood, and that the whole should run:

'From birth, poverty;
For ten years, captivity;
On the seashore, death for a little while;
Happiness shall follow.'

It is the last two lines that are different. And this must be the correct version, because when happiness came to Gangan it was not 'for a little while'. When the goddess of good fortune did arrive, she stayed in his palace for many, many years.

Eyes of the Cat

I wrote this little story for the schoolgirl who said my stories weren't scary enough. Her comment was 'Not bad', and she gave me seven out of ten.

H ER EYES seemed flecked with gold when the sun was on them. And as the sun set over the mountains, drawing a deep red wound across the sky, there was more than gold in Kiran's eyes. There was anger; for she had been cut to the quick by some remarks her teacher had made—the culmination of weeks of insults and taunts.

Kiran was poorer than most of the girls in her class and could not afford the tuitions that had become almost obligatory if one was to pass and be promoted. 'You'll have to spend another year in the ninth,' said Madam. 'And if you don't like that, you can find another school—a school where it won't matter if your blouse is torn and your tunic is old and your shoes are falling apart.' Madam had shown her large teeth in what was supposed to be a good-natured smile, and all the girls had tittered dutifully. Sycophancy had become part of the curriculum in Madam's private academy for girls.

On the way home in the gathering gloom, Kiran's two companions commiserated with her.

'She's a mean old thing,' said Aarti. 'She doesn't care for anyone but herself.'

'Her laugh reminds me of a donkey braying,' said Sunita, who was more forthright.

But Kiran wasn't really listening. Her eyes were fixed on some point in the far distance, where the pines stood in silhouette against a night sky that was growing brighter every moment. The moon was rising, a full moon, a moon that meant something very special to Kiran, that made her blood tingle and her skin prickle and her hair glow and send out sparks. Her steps seemed to grow lighter, her limbs more sinewy as she moved gracefully, softly over the mountain path.

Abruptly, she left her companions at a fork in the road.

'I'm taking the short cut through the forest,' she said.

Her friends were used to her sudden whims. They knew she was not afraid of being alone in the dark. But Kiran's moods made them feel a little nervous, and now, holding hands, they hurried home along the open road.

The short cut took Kiran through the dark oak forest. The crooked, tormented branches of the oaks threw twisted shadows across the path. A jackal howled at the moon; a nightjar called from urgency, and her breath came in short, sharp gasps. Bright moonlight bathed the hillside when she reached her home on the outskirts of the village.

Refusing her dinner, she went straight to her small room and flung the window open. Moonbeams crept over the window-sill and over her arms which were already covered with golden hair. Her strong nails had shredded the rotten wood of the window-sill.

Tail swishing and ears pricked, the tawny leopard came

swiftly out of the window, crossed the open field behind the house, and melted into the shadows. A little later it padded silently through the forest.

Although the moon shone brightly on the tin-roofed town, the leopard knew where the shadows were deepest and merged beautifully with them. An occasional intake of breath, which resulted in a short rasping cough, was the only sound it made.

Madam was returning from dinner at a ladies' club, called the Kitten Club as a sort of foil to the husbands' club affiliations. There were still a few people in the street, and while no one could help noticing Madam, who had the contours of a steam-roller, none saw or heard the predator who had slipped down a side alley and reached the steps of the teacher's house. It sat there silently, waiting with all the patience of an obedient schoolgirl.

When Madam saw the leopard on her steps, she dropped her handbag and opened her mouth to scream; but her voice would not materialize. Nor would her tongue ever be used again, either to savour chicken biryani or to pour scorn upon her pupils, for the leopard had sprung at her throat, broken her neck, and dragged her into the bushes.

In the morning, when Aarti and Sunita set out for school, they stopped as usual at Kiran's cottage and called out to her.

Kiran was sitting in the sun, combing her long black hair.

'Aren't you coming to school today, Kiran?' asked the girls.

'No, I won't bother to go today,' said Kiran. She felt lazy, but pleased with herself, like a contented cat.

'Madam won't be pleased,' said Aarti. 'Shall we tell her you're sick?'

'It won't be necessary,' said Kiran, and gave them one of her mysterious smiles. 'I'm sure it's going to be a holiday.'

Poems

The Bat

Most bats fly high,
Swooping only
To take some insect on the wing;
But there's a bat I know,
Who flies so low,
He skims the floor;
He does not enter at the window,
But flies in at the door,
Does stunts beneath the furniture...
Is his radar wrong,
Or does he just prefer
Being different from other bats?
And when sometimes,
He settles upside down,
At the foot of my bed,
I let him be.
On lonely nights, even a crazy bat
Is company.

The Snake

When, after days of rain,
The sun appears,
The snake emerges,
Green-gold on the grass.
Kept in so long,
He basks for hours,
Soaks up the hot bright sun.
Knowing how shy he is of me,
I walk a gentle pace,
Letting him doze in peace.
But to the snake, earth-bound,
Each step must sound like thunder.
He glides away,
Goes underground.
I've known him for some years:
A harmless green grass-snake,
Who, when he sees me on the path,
Uncoils and disappears.

The Owl

At night, when all is still,
The forest's sentinel
Glides silently across the hill
And perches in an old pine tree.
A friendly presence his!
No harm can come
From a night bird on the prowl.
His cry is mellow,
Much softer than a peacock's call.
Why then this fear of owls
Calling in the night?
If men must speak,
Then owls must hoot—
They have the right.
On me it casts no spell:
Rather, it seems to cry,
'The night is good—all's well, all's well.'

Butterfly Time

April showers
Bring swarms of butterflies
Streaming across the valley
Seeking sweet nectar.
Yellow, gold, and burning bright,
Red and blue and banded white.
To my eyes they bring delight!
Theirs a long and arduous flight,
Here today and off tomorrow,
Floating on, bright butterflies,
To distant bowers.
For Nature does things in good order:
And birds and butterflies recognize
No man-made border.

Firefly in My Room

Last night, as I lay sleepless
In the summer dark
With window open to invite a breeze,
Softly a firefly flew in
And circled round the room
Twinkling at me from floor or wall
Or ceiling, never long in one place,
But lighting up little spaces...
A friendly presence, dispelling
The settled gloom of an unhappy day.
And after it had gone, I left
The window open, just in case
It should return.

Make Room for Elephants

I know the world's a crowded place,
And elephants do take up space,
But if it makes a difference, Lord,
I'd gladly share my room and board.
A baby elephant would do....
But, if he brings his mother too,
There's Dad's garage. He wouldn't mind.
To elephants he's more than kind.
But I wonder what our Mum would say
If the elephant's father came to stay!

God Save the Beetle

Lord, please give some sense of direction to this beetle
Who keeps blundering through the open window
And falling into the goldfish bowl.
Twice I have kept him from drowning
And returned him to the garden;
But he keeps coming back
Zooming and diving about the room, until
P-L-O-P!
He's in the goldfish bowl again,
Swimming round and round and looking very tired.
In five minutes' time I must go to bed
And if you don't get this beetle
To look after himself, who will?
Besides, it makes the goldfish nervous.

To the Indian Foresters

You are the quiet men who do not boast
Although you've done much more than most
To make this land a sea of green
From here to far Cape Comorin.
Without your help to Nature's thrust,
This land would be a bowl of dust.
A land without its forest wealth
Must suffer a decline in health,
For herbs and plants all need green cover
Before they help the sick recover.
And we need trees to hold together
Beasts, and birds of every feather,
And leaves to help the air smell sweet;
All this and more is no mean feat.
Dear foresters, you have not sought for fame or favour,
Yours has been a love of labour.
Our thanks! Instead of desert sand
You've given us this green and growing land.

(Composed and read to a gathering of young forest officers at the Forest
Research Institute, on 10 April 2004)

Tigers Forever

May there always be tigers
In the jungles and tall grass.
May the tiger's roar be heard,
May his thunder
Be known in the land.
At the forest pool, by moonlight,
May he drink and raise his head,
Scenting the night wind.
May he crouch low in the grass
When the herdsmen pass,
And slumber in dark caverns
When the sun is high.
May there always be tigers.
But not so many, that one of them
Might be tempted to come into my room
In search of a meal!

Listen!

Listen to the night wind in the trees,
Listen to the summer grass singing;
Listen to the time that's tripping by,
And the dawn dew falling.
Listen to the moon as it climbs the sky,
Listen to the pebbles humming;
Listen to the mist in the trembling leaves,
And the silence calling.